The Ink That Remains

The stories we keep define the future we build

Tumblebrook Mysteries
Book 3

Ellen Le Teace

Bradford
Press

Chapter 1

Murder at the Book Fair

The morning dawned with the gentle promise of spring, casting a golden hue over Tumblebrook's cobblestone streets. Dew sparkled on the flowerbeds lining the charming town, their vibrant colors glowing softly beneath the rising sun. Amelia Farnsworth breathed deeply, savoring the crisp air as she stepped onto the wraparound porch of the Tumblebrook Inn. Today was no ordinary day—it was the annual Tumblebrook Book Fair, an event Amelia looked forward to with childlike excitement every year.

She adjusted the floral apron tied loosely around her waist, its cheerful pattern matching her mood, and glanced down at her beloved companion, Lady Grey. The British Shorthair cat rubbed languidly against her ankles, eyes gleaming mischievously as if she shared Amelia's anticipation.

"Ready to greet the day, Lady Grey?" Amelia asked, leaning down to scratch gently behind the cat's ears. Lady Grey responded with a soft chirrup, tail flicking elegantly, amused by the unnecessary question.

Guests bustled past, smiling warmly and waving as they made their way toward the town square, already buzzing with life and cheerful chatter. Amelia followed leisurely, absorbing the excited energy of the townspeople as they gathered beneath colorful banners and tents bursting with books of every imaginable genre. She felt a familiar thrill of delight, knowing the entire town would be united today by their shared love of stories.

The fair sprawled across the town's central square, filled with quaint booths manned by familiar faces. In one corner, Mrs. Blakely proudly displayed her famous collection of romance novels, their covers adorned with dramatic illustrations of lovers entwined. Near the bubbling stone fountain, Tom Jensen demonstrated the delicate art of book restoration, his weathered hands skillfully handling centuries-old volumes with reverent care. But most anticipated of all was Eleanor Perkins' tent, housing rare and beloved tomes borrowed from the prestigious Tumblebrook Library.

Amelia paused, appreciating the nostalgic charm surrounding her. The enticing aromas of fresh-baked pastries and rich coffee wafted from the nearby café, mingling perfectly with the faint, comforting scent of aged paper. She felt a deep sense of pride and gratitude for her community, where neighbors truly knew and cared for one another.

"Amelia!" called Clara Henderson, hurrying toward her from a booth filled with neatly arranged mystery novels. Amelia smiled broadly, relieved and delighted to see her friend's familiar, composed expression amidst the bustling fair.

"Clara," Amelia replied warmly, hugging her briefly. "Busy day at the bookstore tent, I imagine?"

"Always," Clara laughed, smoothing her apron. "But I promised Eleanor I'd help her arrange the rare collections today. She's been fussing over them for weeks."

Amelia chuckled. Eleanor Perkins, Tumblebrook's esteemed librarian, took immense pride in her displays, each year growing more extravagant and meticulously arranged. Her presence was a cornerstone of the fair, her dedication to literature woven into the fabric of the town.

"Speaking of which, have you seen Eleanor this morning?" Clara asked, glancing around. "She was supposed to be here early."

Amelia frowned, following Clara's gaze across the square. "No, I haven't. That's odd. She's usually one of the first."

"I'm sure she's fussing over some last-minute detail," Clara said lightly, though concern flickered in her eyes.

"Probably," Amelia said, trying to dismiss the unease creeping in. "I'll swing by her tent and check on her."

With a wave, Amelia made her way toward Eleanor's green-and-white-striped tent at the far end of the square. Lady Grey followed closely, weaving through legs and accepting affectionate pats from passersby.

As she approached, Amelia noticed the canvas flaps were drawn shut—unusual, given Eleanor's preference for open, inviting spaces. The unease tightened. She hesitated, then pushed the flaps aside.

"Eleanor? Are you in here?" she called, stepping inside.

The interior was dim, the tent filtering sunlight into muted shadows that played across tables of precious volumes. Stacks of rare books lay scattered haphazardly. Something was wrong.

Amelia stepped forward—and froze. Her breath caught.

Lying crumpled on the grass, eyes wide and vacant, was Eleanor Perkins.

"Oh my goodness! Eleanor!" Amelia gasped, rushing forward. She knelt, fingers trembling as she reached for Eleanor's wrist, already certain of the truth.

Eleanor was dead.

Amelia recoiled, her stomach knotting with dread. She stumbled back, breath shallow, mind racing.

"Help! Someone help!" she cried, voice slicing through the fair's cheerful hum.

Within moments, townspeople poured in, their faces shifting from joy to horror.

Chaos erupted. Murmurs swelled. Amelia stood numbly, heart pounding, hardly noticing Lady Grey press close against her.

Sheriff Taylor arrived, his calm face etched with urgency. Detective Johnson followed, his gaze scanning the scene before landing on Amelia.

"Miss Farnsworth," he said, stepping closer. "Please step outside."

Amelia nodded, allowing herself to be led into the stark sunlight. The warmth now felt cold against the heaviness in her chest.

"Amelia!" Clara rushed over, gripping her arm. Her eyes brimmed. "What happened? Is Eleanor..."

"She's gone," Amelia whispered. "I found her just lying there... I don't understand."

Clara pulled her into a fierce hug.

As the crowd stirred behind them, whispers rose.

"Why was Amelia there first?" "She reads all those mysteries—maybe she finally acted one out."

Amelia stiffened. Could they truly suspect her?

She looked back into the tent. Bookbinding tools—bone folders, awls, punches—were scattered beside Eleanor. Carelessly. Wrongly. Eleanor had been precise, always. This was staged.

"Amelia," Johnson called, breaking her thoughts. His tone carried a bite. "I'll need to ask you some serious questions."

"Of course," she said, steadying herself.

Just then, a blur of gray darted beneath the flap. Lady Grey trotted toward her, something in her mouth.

"Lady Grey?" Amelia knelt. "What is it?"

The cat dropped an ornate feather pen at her feet. Silver-handled. Distinctive. Eleanor's favorite—the one reported stolen days ago.

Amelia stared, heart lurching.

This wasn't random. Someone knew what happened.

And they wanted her to know it, too.

Chapter 2

A Past Unearthed

Clara Henderson paced the warmly lit kitchen of the Tumblebrook Inn, her usually composed features drawn tight with tension. Copper pots hung from ceiling hooks, catching amber lamplight in flickers, while the rich aroma of simmering beef stew filled the air. It was a dish she had made countless times, its familiar scent once a source of comfort. Today, it only added to the ache of unease.

This kitchen was usually her anchor. The rhythm of chopping, measuring, and seasoning had always given her a sense of control. Her dual roles as the inn's cook and part-time bookshop clerk suited her perfectly—she lived by systems, by order. But that sense of structure had unraveled.

The annual Tumblebrook Book Fair had ended in tragedy. Eleanor Perkins—beloved librarian, friend, and pillar of the community—was dead. And with her death had come gossip, suspicion, and fear.

Clara glanced at the clock above the stove. Amelia should have been back by now. The delay tugged at her nerves. The image of her friend—distraught, freshly accused—made something fiercely protective stir in her chest.

The door creaked open.

Amelia stepped inside, shoulders slumped, her eyes hollow with exhaustion. Lady Grey followed, elegant as ever, but with an alertness in her amber eyes that betrayed the weight of the day.

Clara dropped the towel in her hands and crossed the kitchen. "Oh, Amelia. Sit down. I made tea."

Amelia collapsed into a chair. "The whole town's buzzing. And not in a good way. Johnson grilled me for hours. Apparently, reading too many mysteries makes me a suspect now."

Clara poured two cups of tea, hands steady. "That's absurd. You're not the villain here. People are scared. They want someone to blame. But anyone who knows you won't believe a word of it."

"I hope you're right," Amelia said, wrapping her fingers around the warm mug.

Lady Grey leapt onto the windowsill and settled in, her tail twitching softly.

"We need more than hope," Clara said. "We need to understand what Eleanor was involved in. Someone had a reason to silence her."

Amelia reached into her handbag and carefully set an ornate feather pen on the table. "She was upset when this went missing last week. Thought someone had borrowed it. But Lady Grey found it beside her body. That's no accident."

Clara picked it up, turning it over slowly. "No. It's either a message, or a clue."

She leaned back, mind already sorting possibilities. "Didn't she leave a pamphlet after the last council meeting?"

Amelia retrieved the pamphlet from the office behind reception. They spread it across the desk. Clara examined Eleanor's careful notes.

"This is about library reform," she murmured. "Digitization. New hires. Program expansion."

"Big changes," Amelia added. "Probably upset people who liked things the old-fashioned way."

Clara nodded slowly. "I've heard whispers at the bookshop. People weren't thrilled. Some felt like she was pushing too hard."

"We need names," Amelia said. "Anyone who publicly opposed her."

"I'll ask Mr. Lark," Clara said. "He hears everything."

At Gossamer Fables, the bell above the door chimed softly. Mr. Lark looked up from his stack of books, eyes rimmed with fatigue.

"Clara," he said quietly. "It's a dark day."

"I need your help," she said gently. "Did Eleanor talk to you about the reforms?"

"Yes," he said. "She had vision. But vision frightens people."

"Was anyone opposed?"

He hesitated. "Marjorie Calloway. She was the loudest. Wanted Eleanor's job, some said. And there was talk of a petition."

Clara's brows rose. "To remove her?"

"Yes. Some thought she was tearing apart tradition."

Back at the inn, Clara relayed the conversation to Amelia, who sat by the fire.

"Marjorie might have had motive," Clara said. "Professional jealousy. Maybe more."

Amelia's expression turned grim. "It's a place to start."

Just then, Lady Grey rose and padded into the study. The women followed, watching as the cat batted a worn leather journal from the shelf.

It fell open. A page fluttered to the floor.

Clara bent to retrieve it. Her breath caught.

"It's Eleanor's handwriting," she whispered. "She mentioned a threat. Called it blackmail."

"Blackmail?" Amelia echoed.

Clara read aloud: "They think I'll cave. But I won't. They have leverage. I have truth."

The fire crackled, the only sound in the room.

Clara looked up. "This wasn't just policy. It was personal. Someone was afraid of what Eleanor knew."

Amelia nodded slowly. "And now Eleanor's gone. But we're not. And we're going to finish what she started."

They stood together, resolve hardening between them. The truth was out there, buried beneath layers of charm and secrecy. Clara was certain of one thing:

They would dig it up.

Chapter 3

Suspects and Motives

The morning sun filtered through the lace curtains of the Tumblebrook Inn's front parlor, scattering dappled light across the polished wood floors and potted ferns. Amelia Farnsworth perched on the edge of her armchair, her second cup of coffee gone cold beside her. Lady Grey, regal as ever, observed from the windowsill, her amber eyes unreadable.

"I know," Amelia muttered, glancing over. "Detective Johnson said to stay out of it. 'A professional investigation,' he called it." She dropped into a gravelly imitation: "'Not a tea party for bored innkeepers.'"

Lady Grey flicked her tail in a decisive arc and turned away.

"Well, that settles it then." Amelia stood, already rolling her shoulders. "We're doing this."

It wasn't just suspicion she was battling—it was erosion. Of trust, of community, of herself. The whispers in the bakery stung more than she'd expected: "She always reads those crime books..." "She knows how to make a murder look accidental..."

No. If she didn't get ahead of the rumors, they'd harden into belief.

She pulled on her olive-green coat, slid her notebook into her satchel, and stepped outside. The breeze was brisk, tinged with pine and lake water. The book fair tents were gone, but their ghost lingered in the muddy grass and bits of confetti. What remained was aftermath—uneasy silence, the hollow space where laughter had been.

Her destination was clear: the library.

The stately brick building loomed ahead, its arched windows shuttered against the morning light. She rang the buzzer.

Marjorie Calloway opened the door a sliver, eyes narrowed. "Amelia Farnsworth."

"Good morning, Marjorie." Amelia summoned patience. "I was hoping we could talk."

"Detective Johnson already asked his questions."

"I'm not with the police. I'm just trying to understand what happened to Eleanor."

Marjorie sighed but opened the door.

The library interior felt colder than Amelia remembered. Books lay in disarray on carts, papers half-sorted. The air smelled of lemon polish and dust.

Marjorie led her to the back office, where half-filled donation boxes stood like unfinished puzzles. "You're wasting your time," she muttered. "Unless you're planning to write your own mystery novel."

"I'm not here to accuse you. But I think Eleanor's death might be tied to something she was involved in here."

Marjorie lowered herself into the creaky desk chair. "She made enemies, if that's what you're digging for. Pushed changes no one wanted. Treated us like we were all stuck in the past."

Amelia raised an eyebrow. "You didn't agree with her vision?"

"I challenged her," Marjorie said. "I didn't kill her."

"I didn't say you did. But opposition builds pressure. If someone cracked—"

"She wasn't just fighting over books." Marjorie's voice dropped. "There were budget conflicts. Heated meetings. People with stakes."

"Anyone specific?"

Marjorie hesitated. "Raymond Leach."

Amelia frowned. "The handyman?"

"He was more than that. They were... close. Until she humiliated him last year—turned him down in front of a crowd."

The memory stirred: the book fair, Eleanor on the library steps, Raymond's bouquet trembling in his hand.

"She said he was too simple-minded," Marjorie added. "Too provincial."

That kind of wound left a scar.

Amelia thanked her and stepped into the overcast morning. A bitter rivalry. A spurned suitor. Tumblebrook wasn't the town she thought she knew.

She headed toward Raymond's cottage on the edge of town. The yard was cluttered with chopped wood and rusted tools. The man who answered the door looked wary, his flannel shirt half-buttoned.

"Raymond," she greeted gently. "Sorry to intrude. I'd like to talk about Eleanor."

His expression darkened. "You're not the first to ask."

"I'm not here to accuse. I just want to understand her final days."

He stepped out slowly, folding his arms. "She made a fool of me. That's the truth."

"I remember," Amelia said. "It was cruel."

Raymond blinked, surprised by her bluntness. "Didn't expect you to say that."

"You don't strike me as someone who'd hurt her. But you must've known others who were upset by her decisions."

He hesitated. "People didn't like change. She wanted to upend everything."

"Did she mention being afraid?"

"She mentioned stress. Said people were pressuring her. Wouldn't say who."

That matched the blackmail Clara had uncovered.

Amelia thanked him and returned to Main Street, a bank of

clouds gathering above. As she neared the bakery, a figure stepped from a narrow alley.

Harold Temple.

"Amelia." His voice was low, clipped.

She tensed. "Harold."

"I hear you've been asking around. Stirring things up."

"I'm seeking the truth."

"Let the professionals handle it."

"They don't seem in a hurry."

Harold stepped closer. "You're playing with fire. This isn't a storybook. People get hurt."

She stared him down. "Was that a threat?"

"It's advice." His eyes were cold. "Back off."

He walked away.

Amelia stood still, pulse racing. The quiet of the street suddenly felt menacing. The death of Eleanor Perkins wasn't just tragic—it was dangerous. And someone in town was willing to keep its secrets buried.

Chapter 4

The Hidden Agenda

Clara Henderson wasn't the sort to sneak around after dark. Her world was one of routines and recipes—early mornings in the inn's kitchen and evenings folded into books. But tonight, she crouched beside a lilac bush in the chill night air, heart pounding, eyes fixed on the back door of the Tumblebrook Historical Society.

She adjusted her coat collar and cast a sideways glance at Amelia. "We're grown women. We could just knock and say we're interested in joining."

Amelia offered a half-smile. "And lose the element of surprise?"

"I read mysteries, Amelia. I don't act them out."

"Too late for that."

Clara shook her head but didn't argue. After Eleanor's death, the stolen pen, the blackmail letter, and Harold Temple's veiled threat, sitting back wasn't an option.

They crept toward the basement window—just cracked enough to let the faint buzz of conversation drift out. Clara leaned in, motioning for Amelia to follow.

"...only a matter of time before the police start digging deeper," Harold's voice came through, low and sharp.

"They already have," another muttered. "I didn't say anything. Why would I?"

"You better hope you didn't," Harold snapped. "Because if this unravels, I'm not going down alone. Eleanor wasn't the only one with a ledger."

Clara's breath caught. Eleanor had discovered something. Something Harold wanted buried.

Another voice chimed in—sharper, defensive. "She was asking questions. Meddling. Maybe someone panicked."

"Don't play innocent, Suzanne," Harold's tone cut like glass. "You were the one who doctored the reports. Eleanor found your discrepancies."

Clara stiffened. Suzanne. The quiet, eager newcomer who had ingratiated herself with the Friends of the Library. Clara remembered her hovering near Eleanor at meetings, always offering to help with finances.

"I just cleaned up a few numbers," Suzanne protested. "She told me to—she asked for transparency."

"She didn't know you were siphoning funds."

Gasps echoed inside. Clara and Amelia exchanged a glance.

This wasn't a book club meeting. It was a reckoning.

"Rita sold more rhubarb crumble than that bake sale reported," someone said dryly.

"Watch it," snapped another.

"We're not criminals," a quieter voice insisted.

"No," Harold replied. "You're opportunists. And Eleanor was going to blow it all wide open."

The room broke into overlapping voices—defensive, accusatory, desperate. Clara felt the weight of it press on her chest.

She tugged Amelia's sleeve. "Let's go. We've heard enough."

They slipped away, silent shadows in the lamplight.

"That was more than we bargained for," Clara whispered as they made their way toward the inn.

"We wanted answers," Amelia said. "Now we have suspects. And a motive."

"Multiple motives."

They walked in silence for a stretch, the streets empty but taut. As they passed the square, the soft trickle of the fountain provided eerie background music.

Back at the inn, Clara made straight for the kitchen. "Chamomile. Stat."

Amelia nodded and started up the stairs. "I'll change and—"

She froze halfway up.

"What is it?" Clara asked.

Amelia bent and picked up a folded envelope resting just outside her door.

No address. No name. Just a single line in red ink:

Stay Quiet.

Clara hurried up the stairs, her heart hammering. Amelia opened the note—blank inside.

Someone had been inside.

"I locked the front," Clara whispered.

"They knew we were out," Amelia said. "They're watching."

The inn, once their haven, now felt vulnerable. As if the town itself had turned its gaze.

Clara looked at the note again. "They're scared."

Amelia nodded. "Because we're close."

And just like that, any illusion of safety evaporated. Whatever was hiding beneath Tumblebrook's cozy charm had teeth.

Chapter 5

The Heart of Tumblebrook

Mornings at the Tumblebrook Inn usually hummed with the comforting cadence of routine—clinking teacups, laughter over toast, the low murmur of stories exchanged over breakfast. But today, that rhythm carried a sharper edge. There were glances, carefully worded questions, and silences that lingered too long. Even the hearth's fire, normally so inviting, struggled to warm the heavy atmosphere.

Amelia Farnsworth moved between tables with a practiced smile, topping off mugs, complimenting scarves, answering gently phrased inquiries with vague optimism. Lady Grey slinked between chairs like a silent sentinel, pausing here and there, watching guests with a measured stillness. She had become more than the inn's mascot—she was its barometer.

Despite the tension rippling through Tumblebrook, Amelia's regular guests remained steadfast. A few left handwritten notes tucked under napkins. One read simply: We believe in you.

It bolstered her. Gave her clarity.

The note left at her door—Stay Quiet—was no longer a threat. It was fuel. If someone thought scaring her would send her retreating into the wallpaper, they hadn't been paying attention.

After breakfast service, she slipped into her office to revisit her growing case notebook. She'd started a system: red tabs for motive, blue for opportunity, green for alibi gaps. Clara had even contributed a few theories, complete with cross-references to bake sale records and meeting minutes.

She paused over one tab she hadn't dared touch until now: Sheriff Taylor.

He was a childhood friend. Fair-minded, even-tempered. But he wore the badge. And in a town this small, loyalty often tangled with politics. Still, if she wanted clarity, she had to risk asking.

The sheriff's office, tucked between the barber and general store, smelled faintly of old leather and stronger coffee. Taylor looked up from his paperwork with a half-smile.

"Full house at the inn?" he asked.

"For now," Amelia replied. "But I'm here about something else."

She laid the note on his desk.

Taylor's face darkened. "You want me to launch a formal threat investigation?"

"I want to know what Eleanor told you before she died."

He leaned back in his chair. "She came to me three weeks ago. Said the Friends of the Library funds weren't adding up. She suspected laundering. Asked me to wait until she had the full ledger. Promised she'd go public after the book fair."

"You think she was silenced?"

"I think someone panicked."

Amelia took a breath. "Did she mention names?"

"Only one—Harold. She said he was too smooth for her liking."

"That checks out," Amelia said, recounting what Clara had overheard at the secret book club meeting.

Taylor tapped the edge of the note. "Then you're getting close. Be careful, Amelia. Whoever left this doesn't want truth—they want silence."

She left the office with her mind racing and her resolve hardening. The spring air carried the scent of hyacinths and the sound of bicycle wheels. But the town felt like a chessboard—pieces moving in shadows.

She spotted Pippa, the town's animated florist, arranging bouquets by her cart.

"Amelia!" Pippa called. "You look like a woman searching for answers."

"I was hoping you might have one or two."

Pippa smiled. "Always. About Eleanor?"

"She mention any... relationships? Visitors?"

Pippa's eyes sparkled. "Ah. The gentleman in the green coat. Last summer. Came out of nowhere. Said he was doing historical research. Eleanor wouldn't say much, but the two of them had chemistry. And then he disappeared."

"Library-connected?"

"Spent hours there. Always at opening."

"Name?"

"None she gave. She said some flowers were best left unplucked."

Amelia blinked. "Poetic."

"Everything she was."

Back at the inn, dusk was settling in. The lamps glowed warm behind their curtains.

Clara burst through the hall, breathless. "You need to see this. Now."

Amelia followed her out the side door, down the alley, toward the back of the library.

"The side door was unlocked," Clara whispered. "And I found something."

She led Amelia through a dim hallway to a wall of old portraits. One frame was slightly off-kilter. Behind it: a narrow door.

"That's not in the blueprints," Amelia said.

Clara opened it. A steep stairwell led into darkness.

They descended, flashlights cutting through layers of dust. At the base: a cramped stone room. A desk. Scattered papers. Diagrams. Surveillance photos. Journals.

"Eleanor's handwriting," Clara whispered.

Names. Meeting logs. Maps of library passageways.

Amelia flipped to the final page of a worn notebook.

One name circled in red:

Harold Temple.

Chapter 6

Secrets Within the Stacks

The lantern's beam flickered across the narrow stone corridor, casting dancing shadows along the damp, time-worn walls. Clara Henderson gripped her flashlight tightly, her other hand trailing the uneven brick as she led Amelia deeper into the concealed passage behind the Tumblebrook Library. Silence pressed in, broken only by the thud of their boots on stone and the occasional creak of settling timber above.

Clara's thoughts moved faster than her feet. Eleanor's secret office. The surveillance. The bulletin board. The coded journals. This wasn't the work of a curious librarian. Eleanor had been unraveling something woven into the very foundation of the town.

"Watch the step here," Clara whispered. "Loose tile."

"Got it," Amelia replied softly. Lady Grey moved beside them like a silver shadow, her presence grounding and eerily composed.

The room felt heavier this time—as if it had absorbed their understanding from the night before. Everything inside hummed with tension, with unspoken truths begging to be unearthed.

The wall of pinned papers stretched before them—photos, articles, handwritten notes, strings linking names they recognized. Harold Temple. Suzanne. Rita. Even Sheriff Taylor.

Clara stepped closer. "She was building a case," she murmured.

Amelia nodded. "Not just for herself. This was meant to be shared."

At the center: a City Council document titled Privatization Proposal, pinned beneath a scrawl in bold ink—Gatekeepers of Truth.

"She knew," Amelia whispered. "The library wasn't just about books. It was power."

Clara sorted through folders labeled Whistleblower Strategy, Donor Discrepancies, Meeting Logs. A drawer revealed correspondence with a state-level auditor. Another held bank statements marked by questionable withdrawals.

Atop a dusty shelf, Clara found a hollowed-out encyclopedia. Inside, a flash drive labeled E.

"We take this," she said. "And the critical documents. The rest stays."

But it was Eleanor's spiral-bound journal that dealt the heaviest blow. The entries were frantic, raw:

"The Hammer came again. I told him I wouldn't alter my numbers. He smiled and reminded me who funds restoration grants."

Clara felt her stomach turn.

"Whoever 'The Hammer' is," she said, "he wasn't negotiating. He was threatening her."

"Not Harold," Amelia replied. "Too measured."

Clara's gaze landed on a grainy photo pinned near the top of the board—an unfamiliar older man in a charcoal blazer.

"Who is he?"

A red annotation beneath it read: County Liaison – Reappearance in March. Grant Approvals Delayed. Connection?

A third drawer revealed real estate contracts—not for the library, but for adjacent parcels tied to development zones.

"This wasn't about the library," Clara breathed. "It was a full-scale land acquisition. A quiet rebranding of Tumblebrook."

They worked quickly, gathering what they could.

Halfway up the stairs, Clara stopped.

A sound.

Footsteps.

Not theirs.

She held her breath. Lady Grey crouched, tail rigid.

"Who's there?" Amelia called.

Silence.

Then retreating steps.

They weren't alone.

Someone knew they had been there.

And worse—someone might already be coming back.

Chapter 7

New Leads, Old Fears

The morning after their descent into Eleanor's hidden chamber brought with it a strange mix of adrenaline and fatigue. Amelia Farnsworth hadn't slept. She'd lain in bed, eyes wide, replaying every inch of that secret room—Eleanor's evidence board, the ledger notes, the flash drive. The implications crawled along her skin like static.

Clara had managed better, channeling her nerves into motion. She'd stayed up late cataloging files, backing up the drive, and drafting a timeline. The clarity in her methodical focus mirrored the storm of determination stirring in Amelia's heart.

Now, Amelia stood in the garden, hands wrapped around a mug of Earl Grey. Lady Grey prowled near the hydrangeas, her movements sharper than usual. Alert. Aware. She was always more than a cat—this morning, she seemed like an omen.

Spring had reached full bloom, but Amelia saw rot beneath the blossoms. Tumblebrook's facade had cracked. Secrets were seeping through.

When Clara joined her with a grimace and messenger bag slung across her chest, Amelia offered a quiet nod.

"To interrogate Marjorie Calloway before caffeine? Cruel," Clara muttered, then added, "Let's go."

The town looked deceptively ordinary as they walked. Children played, shops opened, and the scent of coffee drifted from the café—but to Amelia, it all felt staged. Like an old film reel trying to keep its corners from burning.

At the library, Marjorie Calloway sat behind the front desk, looking both irritated and exhausted. Her voice was brittle as ice.

"If you're here to accuse me again, leave."

"We're here for help," Amelia said calmly.

Clara added, "We found Eleanor's research. The privatization plan. The council documents. We know."

Marjorie froze. Her jaw tightened. Then, slowly, she opened a drawer and produced a crumpled envelope.

"No name. No return address. Just this."

Inside was a typed message: Do nothing. Let the plans proceed.

"Did you tell anyone?" Clara asked.

Marjorie's voice cracked. "No. I'm not Eleanor. I don't want to die."

"But you took her place," Amelia pointed out.

"Because someone had to," Marjorie snapped. "Maybe I can mitigate the damage from the inside."

Her silence said everything—not indifference, but fear.

Outside, Clara frowned. "She's scared. But she might still be useful."

Amelia nodded. "Let's try Raymond."

Raymond Leach's home was a garden of disrepair. Wind chimes tangled in the breeze, overgrown roses choked the fence, and the porch sagged under its own weight. When he answered the door, shirtless and blinking, his disheveled state mirrored his wary expression.

"What now?"

"We need clarity," Amelia said evenly.

He sighed. "Eleanor was brilliant. Too good. Too honest."

Clara pressed, "Then why keep shadowing her after she rejected you?"

"I needed her help for a grant. She pulled away when she found out about my old charge—intimidation. Years ago."

"You said she held the key to your future," Clara said. "Did that make you angry?"

Raymond's face hardened. "I didn't kill her. I never even saw her that day. I just wanted her respect. I wasn't enough. That's all."

It didn't clear him, but it didn't implicate him either.

As they turned to leave, a sharp meow sliced the air. Lady Grey darted from the hedges, tail stiff, and circled a bush.

Clara knelt, parting the branches.

A soaked envelope lay beneath the leaves.

Amelia lifted it with trembling fingers. On the front, in Eleanor's elegant hand, was her name.

Inside: a legal document.

Clara read aloud.

"Eleanor's last will and testament."

Chapter 8

Conflict Beyond the Grave

Clara Henderson had opened many books in her life, but few had filled her with such trepidation as the weather-worn envelope now lying between her and Amelia. They sat at the inn's breakfast table, curtains drawn against the morning sun, a hush settling over the room like dust in an unopened attic. Lady Grey perched silently at the window, her amber eyes trained on the inn's front door, as if anticipating someone—or something.

The envelope, pulled from the hedgerow outside Raymond's house, was unmistakably Eleanor's doing. Her handwriting marked the parchment with delicate authority. Neither Clara nor Amelia moved to open it right away. It felt sacrilegious, somehow—like tearing away the last veil of privacy from a woman who had already given so much.

Finally, Amelia reached forward and carefully broke the seal.

Inside, they found a stack of legal pages: Eleanor Perkins' revised will, dated just two weeks before her death. Clara's breath caught. Her fingers traced the edges of the paper as she scanned each clause and addendum.

"She changed everything," Clara whispered. "Look—she established a scholarship fund. Library sciences, literacy, local education... and this clause?" She pointed. "It prohibits private interests from taking control of the library's assets. They must remain public."

Amelia's brow furrowed. "It directly blocks the privatization proposal."

Clara nodded, her pulse quickening. "This will would've unraveled all of Harold's plans. No wonder someone was desperate to stop her."

Lady Grey hopped down and trotted toward the fireplace, curling beside it with a pointed flick of her tail.

"She knew it was risky," Clara murmured. "That's why she never filed it. Or maybe she tried—and someone stopped her."

"We need to find out if the will was ever submitted," Amelia said.

"The clerk's office," Clara replied. "If it's in the record, we'll know. If it's missing... then someone's covering it up."

They packed the documents and slipped out the back of the inn, walking briskly with heads low. Clara clutched her messenger bag like a life preserver. The spring air couldn't shake the feeling that they were being watched.

Tumblebrook looked serene—too serene. Mr. Lark gave a half-hearted wave from Gossamer Fables, but his eyes were cautious. The town's warmth had soured. Suspicion lingered beneath the cobblestones.

At the sandstone town hall, a handwritten sign met them at the door: Closed Until Further Notice. Emergency Repairs.

Clara's hands curled into fists. "This isn't real. There are no crews. No equipment."

"They shut it down to block the will," Amelia said flatly. "Someone in the town office is involved."

They didn't speak as they walked back down the street. Clara's mind buzzed with possibilities—clerks, council members, library board allies. Anyone could be helping to bury the truth.

"We can't trust official channels," Clara said quietly.

Amelia hesitated. "We need someone close to the system, but not loyal to it. Someone scared enough to act."

"Marjorie," Clara said.

"She's bristly, but not blind," Amelia agreed. "She's not the mastermind. She's a pawn trying to survive."

Clara's phone buzzed. One new message: Go home. She's waiting.

No name. No number.

They broke into a jog.

Back at the inn, the quiet felt staged. The fire crackled faintly in the hearth. And then, they saw her.

Marjorie Calloway stood in the sitting room, drenched and trembling.

"I didn't know where else to go," she whispered. "But I have to tell someone before I lose my nerve. What I found—it changes everything."

Clara stepped forward, heart pounding.

"Then start from the beginning."

Chapter 9

The Unexpected Informant

Amelia Farnsworth studied Marjorie Calloway's face, noting the panic etched into every line around her eyes. The proud, combative librarian who once ruled the Tumble-brook Library with biting wit and a backbone of steel now stood in the inn's sitting room looking diminished. Her rain-soaked coat left small puddles on the hardwood floor, and her neatly styled hair clung to her cheeks in limp curls. She looked like a woman unraveling from the inside out.

"You need to sit down," Amelia said gently, motioning toward the armchair by the fire.

Marjorie shook her head. "No. I can't stop moving. If I stop, I might... I might change my mind."

Clara stood nearby, arms crossed, her expression soft but watchful. Lady Grey hovered just beyond Marjorie's reach, tail twitching, golden eyes alert, as if reading the weight of the moment.

"Start at the beginning," Clara said, voice low but steady. "Tell us everything."

Marjorie began to pace, her steps tight and restless. "I didn't want to get involved. Eleanor and I disagreed about nearly everything—her idealism, her reform proposals. But she didn't deserve... what happened."

Her voice cracked. She turned toward the fire, the flickering light casting tremors across her face.

"Did you know about the scholarship fund?" Amelia asked.

Marjorie nodded without turning. "Not at first. I overheard her on a call—someone from the state library council. She said she'd go public once the will was finalized."

"But you were nervous," Clara said.

"Of course I was!" Marjorie snapped, spinning around. "She made it sound like she'd found something. Mistakes in the records. Inconsistencies. Clerical errors I didn't even know I'd approved. And if she spoke up, it wouldn't matter that I hadn't meant any harm. People would see me as part of the problem."

Clara met Amelia's eyes. "Were you complicit?"

Marjorie's face flushed. "Not intentionally. But in this town, rumors don't care about nuance."

From her shoulder bag, she withdrew a slim folder and handed it to Amelia. Her hands trembled as she did.

"I found this behind the drawer panel in Eleanor's desk. Hidden. I wasn't going to say anything, but now I have to."

Inside were pages of annotated ledger copies—handwritten notes in Eleanor's tight script, margins filled with dates, locations, and circled figures. Most of the names were blacked out, but the remaining descriptions were damning.

"She was tracking the money," Amelia murmured.

"And the people behind it," Marjorie added. "Who stood to gain from privatizing the library. Where the donations were really going."

Clara scanned a sheet. "Even without names... 'community leader known for seasonal projects'—that has to be Alden Pike. And 'frequent guest at council planning lunches'—that's probably Brennan."

Marjorie's voice dropped. "It's deeper than I ever thought. And now I know too much."

Amelia looked up. "Are you in danger?"

Marjorie swallowed. "I think so. A note appeared in my mailbox. Three words: Don't be next."

The fire popped. Rain pressed harder against the windows. No one moved.

"You did the right thing coming here," Amelia said gently.

"I'm not so sure," Marjorie whispered. "But I needed someone to know. If something happens to me—"

"Nothing will," Clara said firmly. "We'll digitize everything. Make it harder to bury."

"We should talk to a journalist," Amelia added. "Discreetly."

Marjorie shook her head. "No names. Not yet. I'm not ready for headlines."

"You should stay here tonight," Amelia offered.

Marjorie straightened, a flicker of her old steel returning. "If I vanish from my own home, it'll raise flags. I need to keep up appearances. But... thank you. I trust you more than I ever expected to."

She buttoned her coat, gathered her bag, and walked to the door. "I'll be in touch. Just be careful. All of you."

When she left, silence settled. Clara dropped into the armchair, the folder on her lap. Lady Grey leapt up and planted herself on top of the documents, tail curling around her like a velvet ribbon.

"That ledger confirms it," Clara said. "They weren't just trying to profit. They were rewriting the library's future."

"And Eleanor was the only one standing in their way," Amelia added. "Until now."

Lady Grey stretched a paw over the edge of the folder, as though laying claim to the truth.

"What if Eleanor knew she'd be betrayed?" Clara asked. "What if this was her way of ensuring someone found the truth?"

"Then we finish what she started," Amelia said, crossing to the window.

Clara's phone buzzed.

She checked it, her face draining of color. "Emergency town hall meeting. Tonight. Just announced online. No agenda. Comments disabled."

Amelia's jaw tightened. "They know something's coming."

"They want to bury it before it surfaces."

Amelia crossed to the table. "Then we go. But not alone. We find allies."

Lady Grey let out a low meow, her amber eyes fixed on the darkening sky.

A storm was coming. And it wouldn't wait for the truth to find its footing.

Chapter 10

Town Hall Showdown

Clara Henderson had never seen the Tumblebrook Town Hall this full—or this tense.

The building buzzed with the electric charge of a crowd on the verge. Normally, town meetings were sleepy affairs with lukewarm coffee and nodding heads, but tonight, the air crackled with anticipation. Folding chairs lined the room in tight rows, every one filled. People stood shoulder to shoulder along the back wall, muttering, pointing, crossing their arms in suspicion. This wasn't idle chatter. It was a town on edge, caught between outrage and desperation.

Clara and Amelia slipped into seats near the center aisle. Clara wore a gray cardigan and jeans, blending in, but her eyes were sharp, scanning the room. Amelia sat upright beside her, composed but alert. Lady Grey had stayed behind at the inn. It was too volatile an environment for feline intuition. Clara briefly missed the cat's calm presence, but tonight, their focus had to be absolute.

The town hall, with its high-beamed ceiling and faded flag bunting, felt more like a courtroom than a community center. Harsh fluorescent lights buzzed above. People avoided eye contact. The hush before the storm was deafening. Neighbors who once greeted each other with cheerful waves now eyed one another with wariness. This wasn't just a meeting. It was a reckoning.

At the front of the room, Mayor Calhoun adjusted his tie for the third time in under two minutes. His discomfort was magnified by the restless crowd. To his left sat Councilwoman Brennan, jaw clenched, her blazer pristine. Harold Bennett, chair of the library advisory board, gripped the podium so tightly his knuckles blanched. Behind them, aides exchanged nervous whispers, glancing toward the back where reporters had begun to gather. Camera shutters clicked intermittently, adding to the tension.

Clara leaned toward Amelia. "He looks like he's about to bolt."

Amelia smiled thinly. "Let's make sure he doesn't."

The mayor cleared his throat. His voice wavered. "Ladies and gentlemen, thank you for joining us on short notice. We're here to address some recent... concerns surrounding the library redevelopment plan."

A low murmur rippled through the room.

Amelia casually adjusted her bag beneath her seat. Inside were anonymous packets—copies of redacted ledger pages, typed summaries, and carefully worded questions. Clara had slipped them into the town clerk's mailbox earlier, ensuring they'd be distributed by neutral hands. No fingerprints. No names. Just truth.

Harold stepped to the podium and forced a smile. "There's been a lot of misinformation lately. I want to assure you, any claims of misappropriated funds or secret sales are baseless."

Clara raised an eyebrow. That smile held no conviction. The man looked like he was unraveling.

A voice from the crowd shouted, "What about Eleanor Perkins?"

The room rumbled. Chairs shifted. Voices rose.

Harold blinked. "Her passing was a tragedy, but it has no bearing on the library's future."

Clara felt the rage bloom in the room like a thundercloud.

"And the missing grant money?" someone called.

"What about the zoning permit filed behind closed doors?"

Councilwoman Brennan twitched. Other council members stiffened. The tension deepened with each question.

Mayor Calhoun raised both hands. "Let's keep this civil."

But civil was gone. People wanted answers. Murmurs turned to grumbling, the occasional shout echoing from the back. The mayor was losing control. Distrust simmered.

A young intern walked to the podium, whispered to the mayor, and handed him a set of papers—one of Clara's packets.

The mayor scanned the top page, frowned, and read aloud: "According to this report, an off-market offer for the library property was made three weeks before Eleanor Perkins' death. The buyer was linked to a holding company in Duluth—one associated with Councilman Harold Bennett's cousin."

Gasps. Then chaos.

People stood, shouting. Phones emerged. A woman cried, "We trusted you!" Others surged forward by inches.

Harold stumbled forward. "That's ridiculous! Anyone could have written that! There's no proof!"

Amelia rose slowly. "There are multiple accounts. Eleanor was preparing to file a report with the state board."

Clara followed. "She feared someone was using their position to broker a deal under the table. She documented everything."

"Where is this documentation?" Brennan snapped.

Clara didn't flinch. "It's already been sent to the proper authorities."

Harold's face turned gray. Sweat dotted his brow.

The mayor opened another sheet. "There are annotations here referencing personal gain, kickbacks, pressure to rush permits. I want to know who submitted this."

A voice from the back: "Does it matter? It's true. We all know it."

Whispers became accusations. A business owner stood, pointing. "You came to me last spring about zoning discounts. Said nothing about Eleanor."

Brennan turned. "Is that true?"

Harold stammered. "I... I don't recall—"

"You said a lot," Doris Finch snapped. "Including that this redevelopment would 'revitalize the town.' While planning to cut our history out from under us."

Then, from the aisle, Sheriff Taylor stepped forward. His uniform was crisp, his voice clear.

"I can confirm some of this aligns with an ongoing investigation. Earlier this evening, one of Mr. Bennett's associates—Mr. Russell Marks—was taken into custody. He confessed to forging documents related to the redevelopment plan."

Silence.

Harold collapsed into his seat. Allies shifted. The mayor looked to Brennan. She said nothing.

"We'll recess this meeting for fifteen minutes," the mayor said. "Council members, please join me in chambers."

People didn't leave. They murmured, processed, connected dots. A journalist opened a livestream, catching Clara's eye with a knowing nod.

Clara didn't smile. She didn't gloat. But her heart thudded with satisfaction. They had cracked it open—and more would spill out.

She turned to Amelia. "We bought time. But not peace."

Amelia nodded. "Now we see who runs—and who stays to face the music."

Chapter 11

Rising Tensions

The following morning, golden sunlight filtered through the gauzy curtains at the Tumblebrook Inn, casting gentle stripes of light across the polished breakfast table. The familiar aroma of cinnamon scones wafted from the kitchen—a scent that usually brought Amelia Farnsworth comfort and calm. But today, it felt hollow. The town had gone to bed in stunned silence after the previous night's dramatic town hall meeting. Now, it had awakened into a cloud of uncertainty and paranoia. The serenity that once defined Tumblebrook had cracked, and Amelia could feel the tension in every breath of wind and every creak of the wooden floorboards.

She sat alone in the breakfast nook, her hands wrapped around a steaming mug of coffee. The vapor curled upward, tight and aimless —like thoughts she couldn't settle. Harold Bennett's associate had been arrested. A trail of damning documents had emerged. And the community, once united by tradition and trust, had been shaken to its core. Even the inn felt different—as though it, too, was holding its breath.

Footsteps approached. Clara entered from the kitchen, her apron still tied, her practical bun askew from the morning bustle. Her eyes, however, were keen and alert. She pulled out the chair opposite Amelia and dropped into it with a sigh.

"I just came back from the market," she said. "People are whispering. Clutching their purses, watching over their shoulders. It's like someone turned the whole town inside out. Even Doris barely said more than two words to me—and you know she usually can't help herself."

Amelia gave a slow nod. "I suppose it was only a matter of time."

Clara reached into her apron and pulled out a slim, leather-bound notebook. She slid it across the table.

"I took notes. Gossip, overheard snippets, anything that sounded off."

Amelia raised an eyebrow. "You're becoming quite the investigator."

Clara smirked. "Just observant. You might be rubbing off on me."

Flipping open the notebook, Clara ran her finger down the page. "Mrs. Hemsworth claims she saw Councilwoman Brennan arguing with an unfamiliar man near the post office after midnight. Marjorie is completely unreachable—her house is dark, and her phone goes straight to voicemail. And Suzanne? She's been seen sneaking into the library archives twice this week. No one let her in. No one knows why she's there."

"That's... unsettling," Amelia said. "Why would someone with no formal library role have access to restricted records?"

Clara shrugged. "Unless she has a key. Or someone on the inside. Or..."

She didn't finish the thought. She didn't need to.

Before they could say more, a familiar sound echoed from the hallway—a chirp, followed by soft, deliberate footfalls.

Lady Grey, their regal and mysterious British Shorthair, strolled into the room with the unhurried confidence of royalty. Clenched delicately in her mouth was a curled scrap of paper. She padded to the table and deposited the item at Amelia's feet with a flick of her tail.

"What have you found this time, darling?" Amelia asked, crouching.

Clara leaned over and picked up the paper, examining the faded ink and ragged edges. "Ledger paper," she confirmed. "It's weathered, but... here. This part is still readable."

She read aloud: "'...ward Benn—'"

Amelia sucked in a breath. "That could be the end of Harold Bennett's name. Or someone connected to him."

Clara flipped it over. "No initials, no context. But the handwriting... I think it's Eleanor's. It matches her journal entries."

Amelia scratched behind Lady Grey's ears. "You really do have a nose for clues, don't you?"

The cat purred and leapt to the windowsill, content with her contribution.

Clara tucked the scrap into her notebook. "We need to confront Suzanne. She was cagey when we first met her. Now she's sneaking into archives? Something's off."

"Agreed," Amelia said. "Let's pay her a visit. Nothing too direct. Just... neighborly curiosity."

Suzanne's cottage sat at the eastern edge of town, shaded by two towering pines and surrounded by overgrown lavender. Once warm and filled with music, it now bore Suzanne's impersonal touch— curated flowerpots, wind chimes that never rang, and drawn shades. The windows gleamed with the kind of precision that suggested surveillance, not serenity.

As they approached the porch, the wind rustled the ivy curling along the eaves. Birds scattered from the feeder, startled. When Suzanne answered, her smile was prompt—but too practiced.

"Ladies," she said. "What a surprise."

Clara smiled. "Hope we're not interrupting anything."

"Of course not," Suzanne said. "Come in."

The interior was tidy and stylish, but sterile. It smelled faintly of citrus cleaner. Books on the shelves were arranged like decor, not literature. No photos. No mementos. A laptop rested on the counter, its screen angled away, and a manila folder lay beneath a coaster.

Suzanne offered tea, and they accepted.

"We were just wondering how you're finding Tumblebrook," Amelia said casually.

Suzanne crossed her legs, poised. "Charming. Picturesque. Though... there's definitely a sense of scrutiny."

"Small towns are like that," Clara said. "Especially when someone new starts poking through archived records."

A flicker in Suzanne's gaze.

"I'm a researcher," she said. "Old habit. I didn't think anyone would mind."

"What kind of research?" Amelia asked.

"Community development. Grants. That sort of thing."

Clara nodded. "That aligns with your questions at the book club. All those inquiries about town funding."

Suzanne smiled again—but it didn't reach her eyes.

"Is this about last night's meeting?" she asked. "Do you think I had something to do with... any of that?"

"We think a lot of people have motives they haven't shared," Amelia replied.

Suzanne stood abruptly. "I think that's enough. I have work to finish."

They stood too. But as Clara turned, she noticed a library badge beneath a stack of files. Duluth district. Not local.

Evening painted Tumblebrook in bronze and shadow, but the soft golden hour did little to soothe the unease. As Amelia and Clara returned to the inn, the streets were empty. Windows closed. Doors locked. A town watching itself.

Clara went upstairs to update the guest log. Amelia paused in the foyer, glancing at the mail basket. Bills. Flyers. Junk mail. Nothing suspicious.

Then she saw it.

A note, folded and tucked under the welcome mat.

No envelope. No name.

She unfolded it.

STOP NOW OR ELSE.

Blocky capitals. Blotched ink. Uneven letters.

A chill slid down her spine.

She stepped onto the porch. The street lay still beneath gaslamp glow. No footsteps. No shadows.

But she felt it.

They were being watched.

And someone was nearing their breaking point.

Chapter 12

Shadows from the Past

The next morning broke with a strange quiet—a deceptive hush that hung over Tumblebrook like a held breath. Clara Henderson sat in the back of Gossamer Fables, her hands curled around a lukewarm mug of black coffee, eyes scanning brittle pages of town records from three decades ago. The air inside the bookshop was thick with dust and old paper, the scent of ink and forgotten stories wrapping around her like a worn blanket. Outside, the wind scraped softly against the windows, and inside, the brass clock ticked on with hollow finality.

She leaned forward, scribbling notes in the margin of her notepad. The motion was automatic, but her thoughts were elsewhere.

"Suzanne... who are you really?" she murmured.

Amelia was back at the inn, managing breakfast for the handful of guests brave enough to stay despite the town's escalating sense of dread. That left Clara to chase the tugging thread of suspicion she couldn't ignore.

The name "Suzanne" had yielded nothing in public records. No leases. No donations. No employment history. The Duluth badge

Clara had spotted in Suzanne's home was troubling—and nothing in her background added up. Clara wasn't just looking for oddities anymore. She was searching for proof of a lie.

She turned a page in the oversized ledger. A register of speakers from the town's bicentennial flickered into view. And there, nestled among the names, a reference caught her eye:

"Development in Small Town Economies – Speaker: Samantha Bell."

Clara's heart stuttered.

She stood, careful not to spill her notes, and called across the shop to Mr. Lark, who was thumbing through a stack of rare classics.

"Mr. Lark, do we still have the photo albums from the Tumblebrook Bicentennial?"

He looked up over his glasses. "Archive room. Top shelf, left side. Ladder's a bit rebellious today."

Clara nodded, breath shallow, and made her way past the fantasy trilogies and gardening manuals into the cluttered archive. The scent of time—lemon polish, mildew, ink—clung to everything.

She pulled down the dusty album and carried it to the reading table. Her fingers moved faster now, flipping through parade photos, ribbon-cuttings, blurry candids.

Then she saw it.

A group photo in front of the old post office. Tucked to the side was a woman with unmistakable high cheekbones, sharp eyes, and the same poised confidence she'd seen in Suzanne. But the caption beneath the image read: Samantha Bell, Guest Speaker — Economic Futures of Rural Communities.

Clara stared. The resemblance was undeniable.

"You don't age like that without some serious secrets," she muttered.

She photocopied the image, returned the album, and left the shop with a cold coil in her stomach.

The Tumblebrook Historical Society stood quiet on Oak Lane, a white clapboard house turned archive. Clara stepped inside and was met with the scent of polished wood and old paper. The place felt suspended in time, but Eleanor's absence weighed heavily. She had once moved through these halls with purpose.

Instead, Lillian Mott sat surrounded by paper towers, elbow-deep in archival chaos.

"Clara!" she beamed. "Still chasing stories?"

"More than ever," Clara said, offering the photo. "Do you remember this woman? Samantha Bell. From the eighties?"

Lillian took the image, studied it, and nodded slowly. "She was with a Twin Cities development group. Came through charming as anything, but people didn't trust her. Too smooth. Too... strategic. Returned years later asking about zoning permits and annexation. Left as quietly as she came."

"She's back," Clara said. "Calling herself Suzanne."

Lillian's eyes widened. "That's her, all right. Clara, if she's here again, it's not for tea and memory lane. Be careful."

"Do you remember anyone she crossed paths with?"

"There was talk of a library annexation plan. It didn't fly— Eleanor blocked it. Said it reeked of privatization and control. Eleanor knew how to sniff out rot."

Clara's mind swirled. The pieces were falling into place.

Back at the inn, Clara spread the evidence across the dining room table. Amelia hovered beside her, arms folded, eyes hard.

"She's lied about who she is," Clara said. "Samantha Bell. Suzanne. One and the same. And she's been here before—pushing plans, sowing influence."

Amelia tapped the photo. "She could be here to finish what she started. Or to erase every trace."

"If Eleanor figured it out..." Clara trailed off.

Amelia finished the thought. "It would make her a threat."

Lady Grey shifted on the windowsill, tail flicking once, eyes sharp. Even the cat could feel it—the fragile line between past and present unraveling fast.

Then came the knock.

Amelia froze. Clara's heartbeat quickened.

Amelia opened the door to find Detective Johnson standing solemnly in the doorway.

"Ladies," he said. "We found something. A new lead. It ties into the library's past—and Eleanor's death."

A chill swept through Clara.

The storm they had been sensing for days had finally broken. And it was coming straight for them.

Chapter 13

Deepening Mysteries

The fluorescent lights of the Tumblebrook police station buzzed softly as Amelia Farnsworth stepped inside, her footsteps echoing faintly across the polished linoleum. The building always unnerved her—a space so steeped in quiet tension it felt as though even your thoughts had to whisper. The scent of burnt coffee lingered in the air, mingling with the sterile tang of industrial cleaner. It was a place built on order, but humming beneath the surface was something far less stable.

Detective Johnson waited behind the reception counter, arms folded, expression unreadable. Clara trailed behind Amelia, her gaze flicking across the bulletin board where lost pet notices shared space with announcements for flood preparedness, tai chi classes, and last month's chili cook-off. It all felt absurdly out of place given what they'd uncovered.

"Detective," Amelia said, her voice steady despite the churn of nerves.

"Come with me." Johnson didn't elaborate. He turned and led them down a dim hallway to a windowless meeting room. The buzz of the overhead light pulsed above them like a warning.

On the table sat a sealed cardboard evidence box. Johnson slit the tape with a utility knife and removed the contents one by one—a bundle of documents, a cloth-wrapped object, and a worn, leather-bound ledger that creaked ominously as he opened it.

"This was hidden behind a false panel in the library basement," he said. "No record of it in any inventory. Eleanor found it. She didn't want it falling into the wrong hands."

Amelia stepped forward as he set the ledger down. The pages crackled beneath her fingertips. Eleanor's handwriting filled the margins—tight, methodical, and urgent. Names were underlined, dates logged, codes scrawled in the corners.

"She was building a case," Clara murmured. "Tracing something."

"Not just something," Johnson said. "Artifacts. Historical records. Trade logs and letters—some dating back before Minnesota became a state. Eleanor believed the original library held a private archive passed down through generations of town officials."

Clara leaned closer. "That would be priceless to collectors. And it explains the push for privatization. Someone wanted control."

Johnson nodded. "Exactly. And this..." He slid a brittle envelope across the table. "She mailed this to herself. Likely to protect it."

Amelia opened it carefully. Inside was a faded floor plan of the original library—yellowed and delicate, annotated in pencil.

Clara studied it. "These markings—off the southwest wall—that's not in the current blueprint. Looks like a sealed room."

"Hidden in plain sight," Amelia said.

"I can't authorize a dig without historical commission approval," Johnson added. "But I thought you should see it. Off the record."

Amelia gave a quiet nod. "We'll be careful."

Outside, the wind had shifted. It came off the lake in sharp gusts, like spring had remembered it still owed them winter. Amelia zipped her coat, heart pounding. Beneath Tumblebrook's charm, something deeper stirred.

Back at the inn, the blueprint lay unfurled across the dining table. Clara adjusted the lamplight until every pencil mark glowed.

"If this room exists," she said, "it might be the final piece of Eleanor's investigation."

"And whoever killed her knew that," Amelia replied.

Clara tapped the southwest corner. "If the space behind this wall is hollow, we might access it through the old vents. If we get into the maintenance corridor—quietly—we could confirm it."

"And if we can't?"

Clara gave a dry smile. "Then we improvise. Like always."

The fire crackled softly behind them. On the windowsill, Lady Grey stirred, her ears angled toward the hearth.

That evening, long after the inn had settled into its usual quiet, Amelia moved through the parlor with deliberate steps. Flashlight tucked in her coat pocket, she met Clara at the door. Lady Grey sat poised on the hearth rug, but as they approached, she froze midgroom. Her ears pivoted.

"What is it, girl?" Amelia crouched.

Lady Grey padded forward, tail twitching, and pawed at the baseboard near the fireplace.

"That trim doesn't match," Clara said.

Amelia pried it loose. A cloth-wrapped bundle lay beneath the hearthstone. Dust puffed outward as they drew it free, releasing the scent of earth and aged paper.

Inside were stacked documents tied in twine. Some bore faded seals; others were written in an elegant, looping hand. At the bottom: a wax-sealed envelope.

For safekeeping, should Tumblebrook lose its memory. —Annie Farnsworth

Amelia's breath caught. "Annie... My great-aunt. She ran the inn in the 1920s."

Clara nodded. "She knew. About the land. The legacy."

Clara opened one envelope. "This references a land grant from the 1870s. The original library site was part of the Farnsworth estate. And it says the transfer was never properly recorded."

"If the library doesn't legally own its land…" Amelia whispered.

"Then every contract or redevelopment plan tied to it is invalid."

They spread the papers across the table—Eleanor's notes, Annie's records, the library blueprint.

"This goes deeper than money," Clara said. "It's about legitimacy. And someone killed to keep that secret buried."

Lady Grey leapt to the windowsill, eyes locked on the dark.

The past, it seemed, wasn't done speaking yet.

Chapter 14

The Legacy Unveiled

The fireplace in the Tumblebrook Inn had long been a centerpiece for cozy conversation, warming the bones of travelers and locals alike during long winters and brisk spring evenings. But tonight, the hearth framed more than flames. It had become a passage to the past—a vault of secrets hidden by Amelia's great-aunt Annie, quietly preserved through decades of town politics and whispered rivalries.

Clara Henderson knelt on the rug beside Amelia, her hands gently smoothing out the brittle pages they had found wrapped in oilcloth. The documents, maps, and hand-scrawled notes had the unmistakable musk of long-forgotten history. The edges crackled as she turned them with care, eyes darting across the faded ink, as if trying to read the past one breath at a time.

"This is a boundary map," Clara said softly, her brow furrowed in concentration. "And it shows something that shouldn't be here."

Amelia looked over her shoulder. "What do you mean?"

Clara tapped the center of the map. "The library sits here... but look at this border." She traced a dotted line. "It cuts across the property and clearly defines the land as part of the original Farnsworth estate. Not public land. That could mean the town never legally acquired it."

Amelia sat back, stunned. "So Annie never sold it. Or if she did, the transfer wasn't valid."

Clara nodded. "Exactly. Which means every decision made since —the expansions, the renovations, even the funding—could be illegitimate."

Another bundle revealed a series of personal letters between Annie and the town council of the 1920s. They detailed heated arguments over the town's proposal to establish a library, the resistance from Annie's side, and ultimately, the agreement to lease rather than sell the land. The correspondence brimmed with emotion—Annie's handwritten notes bristled with underlined words, references to family heritage, and concerns over accountability. Some letters bore annotations in red ink from what appeared to be Annie's lawyer, underlining her concern over loopholes in the town's proposals.

"A lease," Clara whispered. "If that agreement was never revisited or renewed... the land would technically revert to the original holder's estate. You."

Amelia blinked. "So the library is... mine?"

Clara gave her a wry look. "In a legal sense, possibly. But more importantly, whoever found this before us would want to suppress it. Especially if they had plans to privatize or redevelop."

They kept sorting, the floor around them a tapestry of revelations. Manuscripts chronicled the town's earliest days—a handwritten memoir from a traveling preacher who claimed to have buried family heirlooms beneath the library's cornerstone. Another document, signed and stamped, warned of tampering with original contracts, suggesting criminal liability. In the margins, Annie had scrawled thoughts, suspicions, and warnings—a woman clearly wary of how easily the truth could be buried.

One map revealed an underground tunnel system beneath the library and town square. A short note from Annie described the tunnel as a former escape route from a Prohibition-era scandal. Clara and Amelia exchanged wide-eyed glances as they imagined secret meetings and hushed betrayals playing out just below the town's polished surface.

Clara found an oilskin folder tucked beneath a dusty ledger. Inside were deeds, hand-drawn maps with coordinates, and a small leather-bound book titled Chronicles of the Tumblebrook Trust. The binding cracked slightly as she opened it.

She read aloud: "In times of turmoil, let the truth remain where roots run deep and history holds breath. For the inn shall keep what the people may forget."

Amelia's eyes glistened. "Annie didn't just hide these to protect herself. She was preserving the town."

Clara gently closed the book. "We have to tell Sheriff Taylor. If anyone can help us protect this, it's him. And if these documents fall into the wrong hands..."

Amelia didn't need her to finish. They both knew what was at stake.

They packed the most vital papers into a waterproof satchel, wrapping it with care, and tucked the remainder back into the hollow. Clara carried the bundle, her arms wrapped tightly around it, as if shielding it from the wind. The streets of Tumblebrook were quiet, fog beginning to roll in off the lake and shrouding the lamplight in a ghostly haze. A crow cawed from the top of the library as they passed by, its echo sharp in the misty silence.

The sheriff's office was only a few blocks away, nestled between the old feed store and the war memorial. As they rounded the corner past Granger's Bakery, the scent of burnt sugar and clove still lingering from the day's batch of gingerbread, they could already tell something was wrong.

The front door of the sheriff's office was ajar, swaying gently in the breeze. The porch light flickered, casting eerie shadows across the threshold.

"That's not right," Amelia said, her voice tight.

Clara stepped forward first, heart pounding, and pushed the door open fully.

The office was a wreck.

Chairs overturned, papers scattered like windblown leaves, filing cabinets gaping open. The coffee mug that normally sat on Taylor's desk was shattered on the floor. It looked like a storm had passed through—a very precise, very angry storm.

Amelia rushed ahead. "Sheriff Taylor?"

From the back room came a muffled sound—a groan.

Clara followed her through the narrow hallway and into the records room, where they found Sheriff Taylor slumped against a cabinet, one arm curled protectively over his midsection. Blood stained the front of his shirt. A thin trail of crimson led from the records safe, which had been pried open and ransacked.

"Oh my god," Clara breathed. "Call for help."

Amelia was already dialing, her hands trembling slightly as she gave the dispatcher their location.

Taylor blinked slowly, focusing on them with great effort. His voice was hoarse. "I knew it was coming," he rasped. "Been getting too close."

"Who did this?" Clara asked, kneeling beside him.

He coughed, wincing. "They knew about the documents. Knew someone would find the truth."

"Who, Sheriff? Who are we dealing with?"

His eyes fluttered, then locked onto Clara's. "Follow the deeds... and watch the council. Not all of them... but one. One of them knew from the beginning."

"Which one? Please, Sheriff. We need names."

But his head lolled slightly as sirens wailed in the distance. His strength was slipping away fast. Amelia grabbed a towel from the nearby cabinet and applied pressure to his wound.

Her eyes met Clara's.

"He said the council. That narrows it, but we need to dig deeper," Clara said. Her voice was steel.

Moments later, paramedics burst through the door, called by Amelia. They moved with efficiency, taking over as Clara stepped back, still clutching the satchel. She looked to Amelia, her expression resolute.

"We protect this," she said. "No matter what."

Amelia nodded. "And we find out who thought they could rewrite the town's history."

The mist outside thickened, cloaking the world in damp silence, but inside Clara felt something stir—not fear, not doubt, but a quiet flame of resolve. Tumblebrook's secrets were no longer buried. And they had the map. The truth had been hidden long enough. Now it was time to uncover the rest of it and bring light to every corner that had been shrouded in comfortable lies.

Chapter 15

Betrayal at Midnight

The ambulance lights cast spinning red and blue halos across the fog-draped storefronts of Tumblebrook as Sheriff Taylor was lifted onto a stretcher. Amelia Farnsworth stood off to the side, arms crossed tightly against the chill, her mind racing. The sheriff had only managed a few words before fading again, but they clung to her like frost on glass.

"Watch the council... one of them knew."

One of them. A name Taylor hadn't had the strength to say aloud —but Amelia's gut told her she already knew. It had sounded like... "Hen..." A single syllable that reverberated in her mind, louder with each breath.

Henley?

Councilman Edgar Henley had been a fixture in town for decades. Jovial at festivals, generous at fundraisers, and always present at pancake breakfasts. But he also had his hands in everything —business permits, building committees, and more recently, a whisper campaign about modernizing the town. If Henley was involved, the betrayal was personal. Deep. And dangerously close to home.

When the ambulance finally pulled away, sirens wailing into the night, Amelia turned to Clara. The satchel was still slung over her shoulder like a sacred artifact.

"We have to get this back to the inn," she said. "It's not safe out here."

Clara nodded. "We hide it where even Lady Grey can't find it."

They moved quickly through the quiet streets, fog swirling around them like ghostly dancers. Tumblebrook felt changed. Windows were dark, blinds drawn. Every sound was amplified, every step a crack in the night's silence.

Back at the inn, Clara retrieved an old flour tin from the cellar—one of Amelia's grandmother's clever hiding spots—and lined it with protective parchment. Inside went the deeds, maps, and the damning correspondence. They buried it in the far corner of the pantry, beneath a rack of dusty wine bottles. Lady Grey sat at the top of the stairs, tail twitching, as if she too understood the weight of what was hidden.

"Now what?" Clara asked.

Amelia looked up toward the lobby. "Now we watch. And we listen."

By daybreak, Amelia was running on coffee and instinct. The inn had a light booking—a couple from Milwaukee, a retired history teacher named Mrs. Tallow, and Greg Withers, a part-time antiques dealer who'd extended his stay unexpectedly. She served breakfast with a practiced smile, but her eyes missed nothing.

Greg seemed distracted. His phone buzzed several times, each time silenced quickly. He guarded it closely. When he mentioned visiting the library before it closed for repairs, Amelia's suspicion deepened. The building had been cordoned off.

Mrs. Tallow lingered over her newspaper, asking casual questions about the sheriff and the council meeting. She mentioned a cousin in Duluth zoning. Innocent, perhaps. But oddly timed.

Even the postman had changed. Usually chatty, he was curt,

barely making eye contact as he handed her a small envelope. Inside was a typed note:

They're watching. Even now. Keep your lights off at midnight.

No name. No signature. No trace.

She and Clara spent the day mapping Henley's influence—permits, acquisitions, committee resignations. The picture sharpened: Henley was orchestrating something. A campaign cloaked in civic progress but rooted in control.

That night, Amelia checked every lock. She fed Lady Grey, ensured Clara was safe, and settled into the parlor with a book she didn't read. Fog returned, cloaking the inn. Shadows danced on the porch. The air felt heavy with watchfulness.

At 11:50 p.m., Amelia crept to the attic.

Clara was waiting, two mugs of tea and the original library map between them. They sat under the slanted ceiling, breath visible in the cold air.

"If Henley's involved," Clara said, "he has help. Records, banking, something."

"Eleanor mentioned a key," Amelia said. "Not directly. But in her notebook—a safe deposit."

As if on cue, Amelia's phone buzzed.

No caller ID. One word: KEY.

She answered. Static. Then a hurried voice:

"You want the truth? Find Box 317. Eleanor left it for you. But hurry. They know."

The line went dead.

Clara stared. "Who was it?"

Amelia lowered the phone. "Eleanor's safe deposit box. It still exists."

Then a shadow passed beneath the streetlamp. A figure paused, looking straight at the attic window. Lady Grey growled low from the corner.

"Someone's watching," Clara whispered.

Amelia peeked through the curtain. The figure was gone.

"If we go to the bank, we need to be careful," Clara said. "We act normal. No panic."

Amelia nodded. "Agreed, but we must guard the documents, and watch Henley."

The clock struck midnight. The inn held its breath.

Morning would bring answers. Or danger. Or both.

Chapter 16

A Test of Trust

The sun rose reluctantly over Tumblebrook, casting a bruised purple hue across the horizon as though the sky, too, bore the weight of secrets. Clara Henderson stood by the window of her small quarters at the inn, watching the pale light push shadows out of corners. Her tea had gone cold in her hands, untouched, as her mind turned over everything they'd discovered the night before.

A safe deposit box. A hidden ledger. A name nearly whispered. Henley.

And now, a decision to make.

She glanced over her notes spread across her small desk—Eleanor's coded writings, annotations in the margins of her journals, maps with pinpricks and coffee-stained corners. It was too much for two people alone. They needed help. The right help. And strangely enough, Clara knew exactly who to turn to.

Marjorie Calloway.

Since Eleanor's death, they'd formed a fragile truce. The prickly former librarian had surprised them both with her tearful confession—and the damning ledger she'd produced from Eleanor's desk. Clara had sensed regret. Real, human regret. A desperate desire to clear her name, and perhaps, for once, stand on the right side of history.

She met Amelia in the kitchen as the morning bustle began—eggs cracking, kettles whistling, and the scent of cinnamon biscuits perfuming the air.

"We need Marjorie," Clara said simply, sliding into the booth by the pantry.

Amelia raised an eyebrow. "To help with the bank?"

Clara nodded. "She knew Eleanor better than most. Their rivalry masked something deeper—a shared burden. I think Eleanor trusted her, in her own way. Besides, Marjorie knows how Eleanor thought. If there are more codes or symbols... she might be the one to crack them."

After a pause, Amelia nodded. "Let's bring her in. But carefully."

They found Marjorie tending her garden, a vision in floral gloves and kneeling cushion. She hummed a forgotten melody, her roses blooming vibrantly. Clara noticed the tremble in her hands as she stood.

Marjorie looked up behind oversized sunglasses. "Let me guess," she said, brushing soil from her apron. "You need more than just an alibi now."

"We need your help understanding Eleanor's mind," Clara said. "There's a safe deposit box. She left a clue. Maybe more than a clue. We think it could hold the final pieces."

Marjorie sighed, removing her gloves. "Fine. But I'm not breaking into any vaults. I'm too old to be mistaken for a cat burglar."

Clara smiled faintly. "No vaults. Just insight—and maybe a little courage."

That evening, the trio gathered in the inn's library. Marjorie brought a bundle of Eleanor's old letters—items she'd never dared turn over to authorities. The parchment was delicate, the ink faded, but the tone unmistakable. Amelia poured tea, the cups rattling slightly in their saucers. Lady Grey observed from a high windowsill, her amber eyes alert.

"These," Marjorie said, spreading the letters on the table, "were Eleanor's final correspondences with the council. And this one—" she tapped a folded sheet, "is unsigned, but it's Henley. He always quoted Thoreau when trying to sound noble."

Clara scanned the lines:

"...and when the path diverges between truth and prosperity, it is the brave who choose truth, though the latter builds the finer road."

Her pulse quickened. The phrase echoed one from Eleanor's journal.

"She was leaving us a trail," Clara said. "This is no coincidence."

Marjorie folded her arms. "And if Henley really is at the center of this... he's not acting alone. He never had the stomach for true villainy. He surrounds himself with people who do the dirty work."

"Like who?" Amelia asked.

"People with money. With influence. The kind who don't get their hands dirty but leave messes for others to clean up," Marjorie replied.

Clara traced Eleanor's script with a fingertip. "She was trying to warn us quietly. These letters were her insurance. Her legacy. She must have known her time was short."

At eleven that night, they approached the bank. The lockbox wing, accessed by a separate code, was quiet. Inside, the vault chamber was sterile and still.

Box 317 sat at eye level. Amelia inserted Eleanor's key. With a soft click, the lock opened.

Inside were envelopes, a slim journal, and a red ribbon looped around two faded photos. One showed a younger Eleanor beside a man in front of the original library. The other, more recent—Eleanor at last year's book fair, with Henley scowling in the background.

They sat on the floor and opened the journal. Eleanor's handwriting filled the pages—some calm, some urgent. The entries revealed a woman cornered, yet determined.

"They approached me again today. Promises of preservation wrapped in veiled threats. Henley leads, but he is not alone. There's a circle—old money and older grudges. They want the land, the legacy, the silence. But I will not yield. Not again."

Clara's breath caught. "She was being threatened."

Marjorie swallowed. "And no one believed her. Not even me."

Letters addressed to familiar names filled the box: Sheriff Taylor, Mr. Lark, Pippa at the florist. Each carried Eleanor's plea: to remain vigilant, to honor the town's roots, and a chilling warning: "If something happens to me, it will not be natural."

Clara found the final envelope, sealed in red wax, labeled: To the ones who kept asking.

She looked at Amelia.

"It's for us."

Amelia nodded. "Open it."

Inside was a note:

"The truth lies not in buildings or paper, but in people brave enough to fight for it. Trust only those who fear power, not those who seek it. The reckoning is coming. Stand tall. Love, E."

Clara folded the letter and placed it back in the box. Her eyes were damp, but her hands steady.

"We have the truth now. Eleanor gave us the roadmap."

Outside, as they reached Amelia's car, Marjorie spotted something under the windshield wiper.

A white envelope. No name.

Inside, a scrap of paper, jagged handwriting:

"You were warned. The final reckoning begins now."

They stood frozen, the cold wind whispering down the empty street.

Clara felt it in her chest: the pressure of time tightening. Their enemy was watching. And the end was drawing near.

Everything Eleanor had predicted was unfolding—faster than they could prepare.

And the next move was no longer theirs to make.

Chapter 17

Masked Allies and Enemies

Amelia Farnsworth had always prided herself on her instincts. Years of running the Tumblebrook Inn had taught her to read people quickly—which guests preferred conversation over coffee, which needed silence, who was hiding something behind a polite smile. But this morning, as she poured herself a fresh cup of Darjeeling and stared out the frost-rimmed kitchen window, she couldn't shake the feeling that someone had flipped the board. That she was no longer reading her guests—but being read instead.

Suzanne Bellamy.

Since the book fair, Suzanne had lingered on the edges of conversations. Eager to help. Quick with questions. And yet, something about her helpfulness felt rehearsed, too perfectly placed. She was always one step ahead in casual talk, always knew just a little too much about things only insiders would. Amelia remembered how, at the town meeting, Suzanne had referenced a historical funding act Eleanor once mentioned in a private journal entry—something only a few would know. That moment had stuck with her.

Suzanne knew too many people for someone supposedly new to town. She blended into the woodwork, always present, never truly noticed—until now.

After last night's chilling note, Amelia knew they could no longer afford to tiptoe. It was time to draw out allies—and expose the enemies pretending to be friends.

She dialed Suzanne's number and left a message inviting her to tea in the solarium. Calm, casual. No pretense. Just tea, conversation, and a quiet place to let someone reveal more than they intended.

Suzanne arrived promptly at two, her scarf a cheerful floral print, her demeanor as bright as the sunlight pouring through the tall windows. Her smile was gracious—almost overly so—and she carried a tin of shortbread cookies as a hostess gift.

"Thank you for inviting me," she said, settling into a wicker chair. "I was beginning to think I was out of the loop."

Amelia returned the smile, measured. "Not at all. I thought it might be nice to catch up properly. So much has happened."

Suzanne sipped her tea, eyes never leaving Amelia's. "Yes, I imagine it must be overwhelming. All this... mystery."

Amelia nodded slowly. "Especially with the library. Eleanor's passing shook the town. And now, with so many conflicting reports, it's hard to separate truth from rumor."

Suzanne offered a look of sympathy. "She was a complicated woman. I didn't know her well, but... she seemed burdened."

"Burdened by secrets?"

Suzanne blinked. "Maybe. Or perhaps just history. Some people carry it like luggage."

Amelia let the silence stretch. She noticed Suzanne fiddling with her bracelet—the same one she wore at the town hall meeting. Antique, with an etched butterfly clasp.

"That's a beautiful bracelet."

Suzanne glanced down. "Oh, this? It's been in my family for years."

"Really? I thought I saw something similar in one of Eleanor's journals. She had quite the interest in local family histories."

For a split second, something flickered across Suzanne's face—a fracture in her smile. She recovered quickly, but Amelia had seen it.

"You mentioned moving here for the quiet," Amelia continued. "But Clara said you grew up just north of here. In Pinemoor, wasn't it?"

Suzanne hesitated. "Yes. That's right. My mother was from there."

"Strange, though. Clara has relatives there and didn't recall the name Bellamy."

Suzanne tensed. "Well, I'm sure not everyone knows everyone."

Amelia let the moment hang. Suzanne drained her tea and stood, mumbling about errands.

"Thank you again," she said, her voice tight.

After she left, Amelia took the teacup and noticed the faint imprint of rose-scented balm—identical to what they'd found on the threatening note.

Back in the parlor, she joined Clara and Marjorie, who were huddled over Eleanor's journal and the materials from the safety deposit box.

"She's lying," Amelia said.

Clara looked up. "You're sure?"

"She knew Eleanor. And she wore a Monarch Society bracelet—the same butterfly we saw in the coded drawings."

Marjorie pursed her lips. "That society hasn't existed publicly in decades. If she has one of those, she's more than just a curious outsider."

Clara turned the journal. "There's an entry. Eleanor mentions a young woman asking about land rights. She didn't name her, but the description matches Suzanne."

Amelia stood and paced. "Then we follow her. Quietly. If she's working for someone, she'll lead us to them."

But that plan would have to wait.

That evening, disruptions began.

First, a burst water pipe under the west wing flooded the linen room. Then power flickered throughout the guest rooms—but not the kitchen. Internet crashed. Phone lines went dead. Not accidents. They were being targeted.

"This isn't coincidence," Amelia said, mopping the hallway floor.

Clara, soaked and shivering, nodded. "They want to isolate us. Slow us down. But we won't let them."

A knock startled them. Greg Withers, the antiques dealer, stood at the door.

"Just checking in," he said. "Heard something in the alley. Probably nothing—but it gave me chills."

Amelia thanked him and sent him off with reassurances, but her gut twisted. Someone was escalating.

They set up battery-powered lanterns in the halls. Clara double-checked locks. Amelia combed through their documents, searching for anything Eleanor might have left behind.

The wind picked up, rattling windows. Lady Grey prowled restlessly.

Near midnight, she stopped outside Amelia's room, scratching at the baseboard. Persistent. Deliberate.

Amelia and Clara pulled it loose, revealing a hollow. Inside: a cloth-wrapped parcel.

Letters. Maps. A note in Eleanor's looping script:

"If you've found this, the game is already in motion. But the pieces are yours to command."

Beneath it: coded symbols, a ledger of names, and what looked like a seating chart. Names they recognized: Henley. Wilder. Lark. And at the bottom, barely legible—Bellamy.

Tucked behind the last page was a photo—a group in front of the library, decades ago. In the corner stood a young woman who looked startlingly like Suzanne.

Same guarded smile. Same sharp gaze.

Amelia's fingers trembled. Eleanor had warned them. That the past would resurface through faces that refused to fade.

This wasn't just an echo. It was a thread pulling taut.

Eleanor had known this day would come.

And she had trusted Amelia to finish it.

Chapter 18

Breaking Through

Clara Henderson stared at the glass-paned front doors of the Tumblebrook Library and drew a slow, centering breath. The air still held the soft chill of morning, and inside, the library's usual hush promised order and calm—but Clara knew better. Within those walls were cracks in the veneer, and she was determined to find where they led.

She stepped inside with measured ease, waving to the two junior librarians at the front desk. The main reading room smelled of old paper, lemon polish, and dust warmed by morning light. The floorboards creaked familiarly beneath her boots. She often came here on lunch breaks from Gossamer Fables, poring over town records or chatting with regulars. Today, however, her role was different.

Today, she was hunting.

Her plan was simple: orchestrate a quiet investigation. She would spread just enough misinformation among select staff and trusted patrons to see who bit. Sometimes guilt didn't scream—it flinched. And in a place built on whispers, Clara knew the right rumor could work like bait.

She started with Irene, the cheerful volunteer who handled the book club sign-ups. Clara approached the table and held up a leather-bound notebook.

"Have you seen the author notes Eleanor was compiling before she passed?" she asked, voice low, as if sharing something illicit.

Irene tilted her head. "Notes? No, I thought her journals went to the historical society."

Clara gave a knowing smile. "That's what they said. But there was another set. She hid them somewhere in this wing. I'm just helping Marjorie catalog anything odd. You know how secretive Eleanor could be."

She let the words linger before moving on.

In the children's section, she repeated a variation to a part-time clerk, suggesting Eleanor had left behind evidence implicating a council member. At the town archives desk, she mused about "certain names" appearing in private ledgers. Always vague, always measured.

By noon, whispers bloomed like dandelions through the library's quiet aisles.

Clara waited. Watched. She made a point to browse at random, linger at displays, engage in idle chatter about the spring book drive, even help an elderly patron reach a volume from the top shelf.

Then she saw it: Curtis Greeley, the assistant who always bragged about staying neutral in town politics, ducking into the far stacks with a determined look. Clara followed at a distance, pausing behind a bookshelf as Curtis pulled out a copy of *Minnesota Land Disputes: 1870–1950* and carefully slipped something behind it.

She gave him a few minutes, then retrieved the book. Nestled behind it was a small black box—a modern recording device, its red light blinking faintly.

Clara's stomach sank.

Surveillance.

It wasn't the first time she'd suspected someone was watching them, but this was proof. Tucked behind town history.

She slipped it into her coat pocket and walked calmly to the front desk.

"I think there's a leaking pipe near the genealogy room," she told the senior librarian. "You might want to check it before it floods."

The librarian hurried off.

Clara returned to the far stacks and began scanning. Behind a reference shelf on railroad construction, she found another recorder. This one wasn't blinking—either deactivated or nearly dead. In the oversized biography section, she found a third. And the fourth, tucked under the periodicals cabinet, had been cleverly secured with electrical tape. A fifth, hidden inside a returned interlibrary loan bin, was more advanced—a directional mic disguised as a faux hardcover.

By the time she left two hours later, she had five devices tucked into a cloth bag. But her discoveries didn't stop there. She noticed Curtis hovering near the microfiche viewer, nervously glancing toward the entrance.

When Clara pretended to leave, circling around the building and watching through the bay window, she saw him make a call—speaking quickly, eyes wide. She couldn't hear him, but she recognized fear.

Back at the inn, she met Amelia and Marjorie in the sitting room.

Amelia's eyes widened as Clara poured the devices onto the table.

"They were listening in the library?"

"At least five," Clara said. "And based on Curtis's behavior, he either placed them or was checking on them. Either way, he knew."

Marjorie looked pale. "Eleanor suspected as much. She thought some of the new hires were too interested in floor plans and less interested in literature."

Amelia leaned forward. "We need to rethink who we trust. Curtis may be a pawn, but someone is pulling the strings."

Clara nodded. "It gets worse. Someone's been rearranging historical records—misfiling newspaper clippings, moving entries. It wasn't random. It was erasure."

"Sabotage," Amelia murmured.

"Exactly. And they were sloppy enough to leave fingerprints. I've worked with the circulation system long enough to know what doesn't belong. Someone's trying to bury the truth."

Marjorie leaned forward, voice tight. "We're not just up against one person. This has structure. Whoever they are, they're trying to rewrite a version of history that benefits their future."

The three women sat in silence, the weight of the conspiracy settling over them.

Then Clara stood. "It's time we visited Harold's associate again. He may have more to say now that the tide's turning."

They arranged the meeting through Sheriff Taylor, still recovering but eager to assist. He coordinated a quiet transfer to an interrogation room in the Tumblebrook Hall of Records. Julian Marks, Harold's associate, slouched in a chair, bandage on his forehead, eyes rimmed with fatigue.

"Ladies," he said dryly. "Come to harass me again?"

Clara stepped forward. "We found surveillance in the library. Five devices. And we know someone's been altering the archives. This isn't petty harassment. It's a cover-up."

Julian sniffed. "What makes you think I care?"

Clara pulled a file from her bag. "Because you left a trail. Bank transfer. Dummy corporation. Account name? H.J. Wilde. We think that's Harold."

Julian stared at the file, his confidence flickering.

"He said it was cleanup," Julian muttered. "Hide documents, misfile deeds. Told me Eleanor was sentimental."

Amelia crossed her arms. "She was a protector. Of truth. Of heritage."

Julian winced. "It was supposed to be money under the table. But once Eleanor started asking questions, Harold panicked. Said she needed a scare."

Clara's pulse quickened. "Was Harold behind the library break-in?"

Julian looked away. "He didn't say. Only that certain documents had to vanish. If she kept digging, there'd be consequences."

Marjorie's voice cracked. "There already have been."

Julian dropped his gaze. "I didn't know they'd go that far."

Clara leaned in. "We need names. Connections. What's coming next."

Julian hesitated. Then nodded.

"There's a network. They call it the Preservation Committee. Sounds harmless, but it's not. They plan acquisitions, push policies, rig votes. All to control which parts of Tumblebrook stay—and which get erased. Eleanor was in their way."

Clara scribbled names, initials, locations. It wasn't everything, but it was more than they had.

Julian reached into his coat. "There's something else. Harold kept a ledger. Lockbox. Votes, bribes, land. He never trusted digital."

They returned to the inn with pages of notes and a rough sketch of Tumblebrook's shadow power structure. It wasn't just the library. It was zoning. Redevelopment. Legacy land sales. Eleanor had uncovered the tip of the iceberg. Now Clara and Amelia were descending toward the frozen core.

Amelia made tea as Clara picked up the phone to call Sheriff Taylor.

But there was a strange click. A second delay.

Clara froze. "Someone's listening."

Amelia's voice was tight. "Hang up. Now."

Clara set the receiver down. The room felt colder. The walls thinner.

Lady Grey appeared in the doorway, tail flicking, gaze fixed on the baseboard.

She meowed.

Clara whispered, "We're not just close. We're at the center."

Chapter 19

The Associate Speaks

The morning fog clung to the streets of Tumblebrook like a shroud, thick and heavy, wrapping the town in uneasy silence. As Amelia Farnsworth approached the police station, her boots echoed against the slick steps, the leather folder tucked beneath her arm feeling heavier than its weight. The town looked unchanged, but she knew better. Change, in Tumblebrook, crept beneath the surface.

Inside, the station hummed with restrained tension. Detective Johnson met her at the front desk, his frown etched deeper than usual.

"You've got ten minutes," he said, unlocking the hallway gate. "He's requesting counsel."

Amelia nodded and made her way to the holding room. Julian Marks slouched in the metal chair, the picture of fatigue and guilt. But his eyes—nervous, flicking toward every shadow—betrayed something more. He wasn't just scared. He was being watched.

"Back so soon?" he said without looking up.

Amelia sat opposite him and placed the folder on the table. Its contents—fabricated financial summaries, blurred photos, and doctored transfer records—were more suggestion than evidence. But that was the point. Suggestion could do what hard facts sometimes couldn't.

"You think you understand what Harold's planning," she said, keeping her voice even. "But you don't know what he'll do to protect himself. You're a liability, Julian. He's cutting you out of the picture."

Julian scoffed, but it lacked force. "You're bluffing."

"Am I?" She leaned forward. "He's already rewriting the narrative. Right now, you're the perfect scapegoat. He ties everything to you, walks away clean, and claims it was a rogue act of loyalty gone wrong. That ledger you kept? He's making sure no one sees it again."

A beat of silence stretched between them. Then Julian let out a long breath and rubbed his eyes.

"You don't know what this town is built on," he muttered. "It's rotten. And Harold didn't start it—he just picked up the reins."

Amelia kept her voice low. "Then help us stop it."

He looked up. "You really want to know?"

"Yes."

Julian sat back, the words coming faster now, like floodwaters behind a breached dam.

"The Preservation Committee. Sounds like a historical charity, but it's a front. They control property, development, elections—even the historical narrative. Lydia Ambrose fast-tracks building permits. Alden Pike gets paid to underbid projects and bury costs. Councilman Leach signs anything without blinking. Bernice Halcomb and Walter Sneed manage the archives and board votes. They manipulate history to protect power."

Amelia's stomach turned. "And Eleanor?"

"She got too close. She found inconsistencies in the town's land records—original grant deeds that were never legally transferred. Old zoning laws still technically in effect. She wanted to expose them. She had evidence."

"And they silenced her?"

Julian hesitated. "The night before she died, I heard Harold on the phone. He said, 'It has to look like an accident.' I didn't think they'd actually do it. I didn't know what they meant until it was too late."

From his coat pocket, he pulled a small, worn black notebook and pushed it across the table. "My ledger. It won't save me, but maybe it can help you stop what's coming."

Amelia took the notebook. It was heavier than it looked. And colder.

Back at the inn, the fireplace glowed dimly against the damp air that clung to their coats. Amelia placed the ledger on the table as Clara and Marjorie leaned in, eyes narrowed in concentration.

"They weren't just hiding corruption," Marjorie said, flipping through annotated library board records. "They were rewriting the town's history. Erasing opposition. Controlling what survives."

Lady Grey trotted into the room with her usual sense of timing, something clutched gently in her jaws. Clara bent to retrieve it—a slim, leather-bound journal stamped with elegant initials: E.P.

Amelia opened it. Eleanor Perkins' handwriting looped across the pages in delicate ink.

"The stories we keep define the future we build. Some truths must be protected, even from those we love."

The journal held more than musings. It was a chronicle: maps of secret meetings, coded names, records of backroom deals, and architectural alterations that aligned with Julian's claims. It even included seating charts of past council sessions, annotated with cryptic symbols.

Marjorie's fingers trembled as she turned a page. "She planned for this."

There was a letter addressed to them—Amelia, Clara, and even Marjorie. Eleanor had predicted the need for allies, not just investigators.

"She left us a blueprint," Clara said quietly. "Not just to uncover the truth. To protect it."

Outside, the wind howled through the streets, brushing leaves like whispered warnings against the windows. Inside, three women—and one watchful cat—pored over the hidden legacy of their town, ready at last to face what Eleanor had feared most:

Not the past.

But those still rewriting the future.

Chapter 20

Town in Turbulence

Clara Henderson stood at the edge of the inn's parlor table, her fingers delicately turning the pages of Eleanor Perkins' manuscript. The soft, yellowed paper crackled beneath her touch, the scent of ink and age hanging thick in the air. Across from her, Amelia scribbled into a notepad, her lips moving silently as she reread passages. Lady Grey dozed beside them, her tail twitching with each turn of the page.

"She didn't just *see* what was happening," Clara murmured. "She *anticipated* it. Every step. Every face."

The manuscript wasn't merely a personal reflection—it was a ledger of warnings. Eleanor used codenames, symbolic references, and layered historical parallels to document how Tumblebrook's foundation had been quietly reshaped over decades. References like *The Triad*, *The Burned Ledger*, and *The Hollowed Steeple* now mirrored real-time events they had witnessed. Some entries read like riddles; others were uncannily precise. Names appeared half-erased in charcoal or hidden between the lines like secrets wedged into the town's very framework.

Clara ran her hand over a marginal note: "When ash rises from clean hearths, look to those who keep no books."

She closed her eyes and let the phrase linger, imagining the town's leadership—each handpicked to maintain the illusion of order while quietly ushering in control. Council votes held behind closed doors, development meetings with pre-scripted agendas. Trust, once cracked, spread like rot.

"She knew about the surveillance," Clara said. "About the rewrites. And she believed someone from inside the preservation committee would betray the rest."

"It's uncanny," Amelia whispered. "She was creating a roadmap. Not for herself—for whoever found this."

Lady Grey stretched, pawing lazily at a page before curling back into a tight, alert loaf. Her presence, oddly grounding, seemed to suggest they were exactly where they needed to be.

The door to the inn creaked open, and Pippa entered, windblown and flustered.

"It's started," she said breathlessly. "The council meeting. People are shouting in the square. Everyone wants answers. It's worse than the library vote. The square's packed, and no one's backing down."

Clara and Amelia exchanged a glance. This was the moment. The tipping point Eleanor had predicted. The crossroads where truth and fear collided.

The town hall overflowed with bodies and boiling tempers. Clara had never seen Tumblebrook like this—cracking under the weight of its own secrets. Politeness had peeled away, revealing years of buried resentment. Even children peeked out from behind parents' legs, sensing the gravity.

Sheriff Taylor stood near the double doors, arms crossed, trying to maintain order with little success. Clara and Amelia slipped in through a side entrance and wove through a cluster of residents from both sides of the dispute. As they passed, murmurs followed them:

whispers of bravery, curiosity, even accusation. The room felt five degrees warmer than outside, fueled by anger and breathless anticipation.

On the dais, three remaining council members sat behind the long oak desk, pale and rigid. Lydia Ambrose, head of development, fidgeted with trembling hands. Councilman Leach mopped his brow. Walter Sneed, the historical society's president, stared into the crowd as if willing it to vanish.

Amelia nodded to Clara. It was time.

She rose first. Clara followed, notes pressed to her chest. Each step forward felt like stepping into a storm.

"Ladies and gentlemen," Amelia said, her voice carrying with practiced ease. "We've come here today with questions—not accusations, not chaos. But Tumblebrook deserves transparency."

Someone in the crowd shouted, "Tell that to Eleanor!"

A murmur followed.

Clara stepped forward.

"In the past weeks, we've uncovered documentation that suggests a coordinated effort to alter records, shift land rights, and suppress historical truths. This effort may go back decades. And it implicates individuals who've had influence over this town's development, budget, and cultural preservation."

Gasps rippled through the audience.

Leach sat up straight. "This is hearsay. There is no proof."

Amelia withdrew the notebook Julian had surrendered and held it up. "This ledger documents payments. Timestamps. Names. And we have corroborating statements."

"Forgery!" a voice on the dais snapped.

"Then explain why the deposits match archival records," Clara countered. "We've matched the handwriting on contracts to council member signatures—including Mr. Pike's."

Another voice shouted from the back, "Are you saying we've been paying taxes to fund a cover-up?"

That turned the crowd.

A dozen more hands rose with questions. The tension snowballed. A woman near the front waved a faded photograph of her grandfather beside Eleanor, shouting about broken promises. A teenage boy stood on a bench, demanding to know who tore down his great-aunt's donated statue from the library courtyard. A retired postman accused the council of selling off parcels of public parkland under aliases.

Councilwoman Ambrose attempted to calm the room. "Let's be reasonable. These are complicated matters that cannot be settled in a single meeting."

"No," Clara said. Her voice did not rise, but it cut through the room like a bell. "These are simple matters. They're about honesty, trust, and whether you've respected the people who believed in you."

She held up a printed page.

"This is Eleanor Perkins' final will. Verified and notarized. It includes a provision for a community trust to preserve library ownership under public stewardship. That trust was overridden without public vote. By you."

Walter Sneed flushed red. "We were advised it wasn't enforceable!"

"By whom?" Clara asked.

The room fell silent.

In the hush, Pippa stood and said simply, "We want the library back. We want our town back."

The room erupted. Some applauded. Others demanded resignations. Clara remained still. She wasn't finished.

Marjorie Calloway, long silent at the edge of the chamber, stepped forward to stand with them.

"Eleanor once told me, 'Truth takes its time, but it always shows up.' Well, it's here. And so are we."

A cluster of book club members took up a chant: "Tumblebrook deserves the truth!"

Even the most stoic council aides were beginning to shift uneasily.

. . .

After the meeting recessed into chaos, Clara and Amelia stepped into the corridor outside the council chambers. They needed air.

The manuscript Eleanor had left wasn't just about what had gone wrong. It hinted, in eloquent metaphor, at how to rebuild. Clara flipped through the pages again, her breath catching as the symbols began to align.

"Look not only to the stone that cracked, but to the seed beneath it. There lies renewal."

"She meant people," Clara whispered. "The people who still care. The ones who didn't look away."

Amelia nodded. "She didn't just leave warnings. She left hope."

And then Clara noticed a phrase scribbled in the margin of the final chapter.

"The three rise, but they do not lead. The true revival waits beneath the badge, the bell, and the bloom."

Clara stared at the words, her mind racing.

"The badge? Sheriff Taylor. The bell—the old chapel, maybe? The bloom—Pippa."

Amelia looked over her shoulder. "It's a riddle."

Clara nodded slowly. "Or a prophecy. A framework for what comes next."

They returned to the inn that night, exhausted but electric. Clara sat at the writing desk, cross-referencing town meeting minutes with Eleanor's notes. Each time she thought the puzzle complete, another layer revealed itself. The floor beneath them creaked with age, but tonight, it felt like it was finally bearing witness.

Outside, the wind carried the scent of pine and the soft crunch of footsteps. Someone was watching. Or waiting. The town was listening now—and not just the living.

Inside, the fire burned steadily. Lady Grey curled beside the manuscript, guarding it like a relic. Amelia sat across from Clara with tea in hand, her expression unreadable.

"We're close," she said.

"Closer than anyone has ever dared to be," Clara replied.

She looked down at the final page of Eleanor's manuscript.

"When truth finds its voice in more than whispers, listen for the sound of rebuilding. It will begin not with celebration, but with conscience."

Clara leaned back, heart heavy with responsibility.

They had uncovered the rot. Now came the harder part: healing what had been broken.

Chapter 21

Unlikely Confessions

The morning fog clung to the windows of the Tumblebrook Inn like a secret unwilling to be parted with. Amelia Farnsworth stood in the sunroom, her teacup untouched and cooling on the windowsill, eyes scanning the hazy street below. The inn remained quiet—almost reverent—after the chaos of the town meeting the night before. But Amelia knew it was the calm before another storm. Every instinct within her whispered that something else was coming, the way clouds always thicken before a downpour. The tension in town had shifted from silence to the sharp tremble of anticipation.

Somewhere out there, Harold and the remaining members of the so-called Triad were regrouping, scrambling to mask what had been unearthed. But the damage was done. The council chambers would never hold the same sway. The manuscript, Eleanor's testimony, and the townspeople's raw fury had shifted the town's center of gravity. Secrets buried deep beneath polite smiles and floral bunting had erupted into the light.

And now, Amelia had to finish what Eleanor started. The truth couldn't remain buried, not when it had already begun to bloom in the open. There was a line between justice and vengeance, and Amelia was resolved to stay on the right side of it—but that didn't mean she would walk away. Not now. Not after everything that had come to light.

She had begun to suspect Suzanne weeks ago. The woman's timing, her seemingly sudden ties to the library, the evasiveness whenever Eleanor was mentioned—it all added up. But suspicion alone wouldn't hold up to public scrutiny. She needed more than intuition. She needed confessions—and fast.

Which is why, at that very moment, she found herself walking down Elm Street toward the modest apartment above the bakery—a small studio rented by Lizbeth Corbin and Penny Madsen, longtime friends of Suzanne's from their university days. Until recently, they had kept a low profile. But now, with tensions high and the town swirling with accusations, their silence felt more strategic than innocent.

Amelia knocked. The knock echoed against the weathered wood, its sound vanishing into the thick fog. Her gloved hand lingered at the doorframe, mind racing. If they refused to talk, she had no plan B.

It was Lizbeth who answered, still in her robe, her eyes red-rimmed and wary. Behind her, Penny hovered in the kitchen, sipping coffee and watching cautiously.

"Amelia," Lizbeth said, voice hoarse. "I suppose this was inevitable."

"You know why I'm here," Amelia replied. "I just want the truth."

Lizbeth hesitated, then stepped back. "Come in."

The apartment smelled of cinnamon scones and lavender—pleasant, almost heartbreakingly so. Amelia stood just inside the door, not removing her coat. The contrast between the cozy, lived-in space and the heavy secret it held nearly made her falter. There were books on the counter, embroidery on the arm of a chair, a cracked windowpane with a patch of duct tape across it. It looked like a place where no conspiracy could survive. And yet...

"We didn't kill her," Penny said quickly.

"But you know who did," Amelia replied, her voice low. "Or why."

Lizbeth slumped into a dining chair. Penny remained standing, arms crossed tightly over her chest, eyes darting between the two. The air in the room thickened as if the walls were leaning in.

"Suzanne didn't want to hurt Eleanor," Lizbeth said slowly. "But she was working with people who did. It was supposed to be surveillance. Observations. Gathering leverage."

"Who was she working for?"

Penny set her cup down, the porcelain clinking loudly.

"Harold. And Leach. The Triad needed someone with fresh eyes. Suzanne had connections through her late aunt—one of the old estate managers. She had access to property records, archived correspondences, the kind of stuff Eleanor was digging into."

Amelia processed this, her mind clicking through timelines, snippets of overheard conversations, and discrepancies that suddenly made sense. Suzanne's hesitations, her blank stares when asked about historical documents, her curated charm at every council-related event—it all aligned.

"You helped her?"

Lizbeth nodded slowly. "We coded the documents she passed on. Eleanor was getting too close to the old transactions. There was a missing deed tied to the land under the library—a deed that proved the original grant never passed lawfully to municipal hands. If that came out, the whole development initiative would collapse."

"You are aware this is my families deed? This is why Harold wanted her silenced," Amelia said.

Penny looked down. "She was never supposed to die. Just... discredited. But then she found the second ledger. The one no one knew still existed. That changed everything."

Amelia swallowed hard. "Where is that ledger now?"

Lizbeth reached under the dining table and pulled out a worn canvas tote. From it, she retrieved a leather-bound journal, aged and cracked at the spine.

"This is what she found. She made us promise not to destroy it."

Amelia took it reverently. The weight of history—and justice—pressed against her palms. She didn't speak. She didn't need to. The betrayal within its pages was already speaking loudly.

That afternoon, Amelia met Detective Johnson at his office.

"Ms. Farnsworth."

"Detective. I have something you need to see."

She handed him the journal. He opened it, skimming, his eyes narrowing. After several minutes, he set it down.

"If I bring this forward, there will be consequences. You know that."

"There already have been. Eleanor paid the price. The town deserves the truth."

"Your involvement blurs some lines here. You should step back."

"I can't. I was there at the beginning. I'll be there at the end."

"The Triad's already cracking. Leach is avoiding calls. Walter Sneed hired an attorney. If I push this to court, they'll try to turn on each other. But I need one final piece."

"Harold."

"He's the linchpin. And if you have a way to draw him out..."

"Then let me set the stage."

That evening, Amelia called Clara, Pippa, and Marjorie to the inn. They gathered in the parlor, the fire crackling quietly. Tension thickened the room.

"Tomorrow," Amelia said, "we hold a public forum. We invite everyone. We ask the council to speak. We present the documents. And we give Harold one last chance to face us—in front of the town."

"What if he doesn't show?" Clara asked.

"He will. His ego won't allow otherwise."

"And if he runs?" Pippa asked.

"Then we follow. And the town follows, too. We don't let him disappear into the shadows. Not anymore."

"Eleanor never backed down," Marjorie said. "Neither will we."

Lady Grey meowed once, sharp and clear, before leaping onto the window ledge. The cat perched like a sentry, her golden eyes reflecting flickers of firelight and purpose.

Outside, the wind shifted. It smelled of rain. And reckoning. And, perhaps, redemption.

Chapter 22

Echoes of the Past

Clara Henderson stood beneath the dusty light filtering through the upper windows of the Tumblebrook Library, her fingers tapping lightly against the surface of the reading desk as she studied a column of archived dates. The library, once her sanctuary of solitude and stories, now felt heavier—its silence thick with withheld truths. Every creak of timber, every whisper of movement unsettled her. It felt as though the walls themselves were holding their breath.

She wasn't here to read. She was here to remember. To uncover. To follow Eleanor Perkins' final trail.

One name echoed through Clara's thoughts: "The Hammer."

It had appeared again and again in Eleanor's notes—scribbled hastily in margins, referenced in footnotes, and muttered in warnings from those who dared speak of Tumblebrook's past. Clara had never believed in ghosts, but she believed in power structures. The Hammer wasn't a person; it was a role—an institutional enforcer, a symbol of old Tumblebrook control disguised as tradition.

Clara dove into the digitized archives, painstakingly curated by Eleanor over decades. The system was clunky, the software ancient, but it housed a trove of knowledge. Eleanor had woven together newspaper clippings, council meeting transcripts, land deeds, and family genealogies with meticulous cross-referencing.

Keywords: "Hammer," "Perkins," "land transfer," "library trust," "municipal override."

Her eyes skimmed entry after entry. A 1979 town hall transcript jumped out:

"Meeting disrupted when Lucille Greaves accused Charles Leach Sr. of altering donation records. Her words: 'Your hammer won't smash us all.'"

Clara sat back. There it was. The metaphor had roots. And Lucille Greaves—Suzanne's aunt.

Next came a 1981 land reassignment. The Perkins family had relinquished a key parcel near the lake—the same area now at the center of redevelopment plans. The document had been notarized by Lucille.

None of this was coincidence. Suzanne hadn't wandered into town by chance. She had a legacy here, one rooted in the very soil Eleanor had fought to preserve. Clara's breath quickened.

Layer by layer, Clara traced the overlapping histories of land transfers, familial alliances, and quiet betrayals. It became clear: Eleanor had been the last defender of a fragile truth.

She ascended to the third floor—the rare book room, still under partial renovation. Eleanor's locked cabinet had been cleared, but one stuck drawer of the old card catalog caught her attention. Inside were pamphlets, protest flyers, and annotated agendas.

A letter surfaced. Yellowed. Creased. Addressed to Lucille Greaves.

"If Eleanor succeeds in transferring oversight to the trust, our hold fractures. You know what must be done. Keep your niece close. —R.H."

Raymond Harold.

Clara felt the ground shift. Harold wasn't a late-stage schemer.

He'd been orchestrating this for decades. The letter was confirmation.

Back downstairs, she passed the research wing and spotted an open laptop left behind. On screen: a scanned image of the 1985 Spring Festival. Clara leaned in. Among the crowd, a younger Harold. Beside him, Lucille Greaves. Both wore pins. But it was Harold's keychain that stopped Clara cold.

She'd seen it recently—on the toolbelt of Carl Tiller, a contractor supposedly fixing piping in the town hall.

Clara left the library and headed to his office.

The blinds were drawn. The side door was ajar.

She stepped in. Blueprints. Coffee cups. Tool kits. And on a hook —the keychain. R.H.

Behind her, the door creaked.

Carl Tiller.

"Looking for something?"

Clara held up the keychain. "The truth."

Carl's smile was cold. "You always were clever. Doesn't mean you're safe."

"Eleanor trusted you."

"Eleanor didn't see the future."

"She saw the truth."

A long silence.

"What will you do with it?" he asked.

"What Eleanor couldn't."

Clara walked out. The bell tower tolled four. Wind curled down the street like breath through stone.

Eleanor had left a trail. Clara was nearly at the center.

Tomorrow, the town would listen. And this time, they wouldn't look away.

Chapter 23

Rumors and Revelations

Amelia Farnsworth watched from the wraparound porch of the Tumblebrook Inn as early morning mist unspooled across the cobblestone streets like a slow exhale. The chill in the air didn't bother her; it matched the tension that had settled in her bones. Every guest who came through her door lately carried whispers in their coat pockets, murmured half-truths over coffee, and cast side-eyed glances at the innkeeper entangled in the town's unraveling mystery.

The book fair had come and gone, but in a town like Tumblebrook, rumor lasted longer than fact. Eleanor's death had shocked the community, then outraged it. Now, doubt simmered beneath every surface.

Some whispered that the truth had been buried with Eleanor. Others, that her death wasn't what it seemed. And a new, insidious story was taking shape—one suggesting Eleanor had secrets darker than anyone knew. It wasn't just gossip anymore. It was weaponized memory, reshaped and fed by the people who stood to lose the most if the truth came to light.

Clara arrived just past seven, bundled tightly against the cold, a folder thick with articles and clippings under her arm. She took a seat beside Amelia without a word.

"They're turning it," she said finally. "Harold's using the Gazette to discredit her. He called the community trust a 'vanity project cloaked in moralism.'"

Amelia snorted. "He couldn't spell 'moralism' if it were written in frosting on a cake."

Clara smirked. "Still, people are listening. We need to counter it. Not with more noise—with something he can't twist."

Amelia opened the folder, flipping through old news clippings and photographs of Eleanor's work—literacy programs, youth mentorship, historical preservation efforts.

"This is the Eleanor people remember," she said softly. "Let's help them remember out loud."

That morning, the idea took root. By midday, they had transformed Doris Finch's café into the headquarters of the Eleanor Archive—a living memorial made from the stories of those she'd touched. With Doris's blessing, they pinned up flyers, set out notebooks, and invited the town to contribute. Notes, photographs, bookmarks, memories—a growing tribute bloomed along the back wall.

Later that day, Amelia and Clara visited Sheriff Taylor with new evidence—the 1985 festival photo, the letter addressed to Suzanne's aunt, and a growing chain of documents linking Harold and Carl Tiller to decades of manipulation.

Taylor studied the items carefully. "What you're doing with the archive—that's smart. People remember stories better than dates. But you'll need more than memory if this goes to court."

He offered the community hall for a public event—a memorial under the guise of a literacy celebration. A stage. A microphone. A place for truth to speak.

They spent the rest of the afternoon canvassing: the school, the retirement home, the garden club. Everywhere they went, Eleanor's legacy echoed back at them. The archive swelled. Children brought drawings. Elders contributed letters. Shopkeepers added drop boxes. Even tourists paused to ask, "Who was Eleanor?"

By dusk, the town was humming with remembrance. Stories passed from hand to hand, across café counters and between shelves at the bookstore. Eleanor had become legend—not because she had died, but because the town remembered why she had mattered.

That night, back at the inn, Amelia climbed the stairs to her room with Eleanor's unopened letter in her coat. She peeled away her scarf and boots, then sat at her desk and read.

Amelia,

If you're reading this, it means I've lost the battle I feared was coming. Don't let the stories fade. They'll rewrite me if they can. Remind them who I was—and who we are when we stand together.

Yours in words and wonder, Eleanor

The letter trembled in her hands. She pressed it to her chest, blinking back tears.

But as she turned down the covers of her bed, something unexpected slid free: a single iron button, rusted and stamped with an emblem she recognized from the Old Tumblebrook Charter Committee. Beneath it, a slip of parchment in delicate, slanted ink:

Keep your stories. We keep the town.

Lady Grey hissed from her perch.

Amelia stood motionless. Someone had entered her room. Crossed her threshold. Left a message.

She picked up the button and placed it beside Eleanor's letter. Then she looked to the shadows and said aloud, calm and certain:

"Then let them watch. We're not done yet."

The battle for Tumblebrook wasn't finished.

It was only beginning.

Chapter 24

Tactical Moves

The Tumblebrook Inn glowed with curated charm, wrapped in golden lamplight, polished floors, and antiques that whispered of a gentler time. But tonight, beneath the veneer of cozy elegance, the inn had become a chessboard—and Clara Henderson had arranged every piece with precision.

Every hors d'oeuvre was handpicked to disarm. The vintage jazz, chosen for its nostalgic undertones, lulled tension. Chairs weren't arranged for comfort but for surveillance—pulling allies together, isolating threats. The faux-historical auction was a ruse, complete with fictional relics like an "ink-stained glove" from a town founder and a cracked compass that "guided the first library shipment." Guests laughed. They indulged. But Clara wasn't here to entertain.

She was here to listen. To hunt.

Perched near the staircase, clipboard in hand, Clara cataloged behavior more than bids. The guest list was a cross-section of Tumblebrook's power—land developers, former council members, library board skeptics, and figures with too much influence and too little scrutiny. Tonight was a controlled burn. And she was watching who reached for the match.

Amelia worked the floor, radiant and composed, spinning tales of the auction's fabricated relics with the warmth of a seasoned hostess. Her performance disarmed. Her grace distracted. But Clara knew the truth: tonight, Amelia was the veil. Clara was the scalpel.

She watched for missteps. Reactions. Councilwoman Avery flinched when Amelia joked about the "waterway negotiations" map. Marcus Tiller lingered too long near the ledger of auction items, eyes scanning—not with curiosity, but calculation. Harold kept to the periphery, polished and evasive, his eyes sweeping the room, avoiding anyone who remembered Eleanor fondly.

Clara intercepted Marcus near the punch bowl.

"Beautiful evening," he offered, raising his glass.

Clara's smile was tight. "History's always beautiful in hindsight. Messy up close."

Marcus blinked, stalled. A beat too long. "I suppose it is."

She watched him retreat to the foyer.

Strike two.

She swept the room again, her eyes cataloging posture shifts, awkward silences, shoulder angles. Guests leaned in or pulled away, lingered or excused themselves too quickly. It wasn't the conversations that mattered—it was the spaces between them. The silences. The glances.

Near the bar, Clara overheard a planning commissioner inquire about "resale contingencies" under the library district clause. Another guest casually dropped the term "site leverage" while discussing the auction's proceeds. Clara's pen flew across her notepad. These weren't idle questions. These were breadcrumbs.

At the event's peak, she slipped outside.

The night air hit her like truth—sharp and unfiltered. Beneath a flickering sconce, she reviewed her notes:

Marcus Tiller: Proxy. Jittery. Possibly unaware of full scope. Avery: Defensive. Agitated by archival references. Harold: Performing. Tracking. Avoiding key witnesses. Unknown brunette in red scarf: lingered too long near archive display. Follow up.

Then—movement. Voices near the hedge line. Clara stepped off the gravel path and crouched behind a trimmed arbor, heart pounding.

"They're losing control," said a younger voice.

"Then we escalate," Harold replied. "Let them toast their saint. The morning paper will tell another story."

"They want a symbol."

"Then give them one. Scandal. Outrage. Let the town turn on itself."

Clara clenched her jaw, forcing herself to stay still. To breathe.

The voices retreated. She darted back inside.

Amelia was guiding Mrs. Polk down the stairs when their eyes met.

"What happened?" Amelia asked under her breath.

Clara relayed the conversation in clipped, urgent words.

"He's planning a coordinated smear. Using outside voices to flood the town with disinformation."

"Then we get ahead of it," Amelia said. "Tonight."

They pivoted instantly. A new layer to the event took shape.

Guests were invited to write memories of Eleanor—framed as a tribute to Tumblebrook's "library legacy." Framed cards appeared on tables. Archival paper replaced auction ballots. Sentiment softened the room.

Then came the audio: Eleanor's voice—excerpts from interviews, public readings—woven into the background hum like ghosts speaking truth.

Eyes misted. Conversations quieted. Even skeptics grew still.

By night's end, the inn had transformed. Stories pinned to the walls. Memory cards filled with truth. A guestbook brimming with signatures—time-stamped, corroborated.

Amelia stood beside Clara in the empty parlor, firelight flickering across her face.

"It was like watching a spell break," Amelia whispered.

Clara nodded. "We shifted the narrative."

She pulled something from her coat pocket—a matchbook. Embossed with a triangle and a flame. She placed it beside Eleanor's sketchbook.

Amelia's eyes widened. "That symbol..."

Clara opened the book to a page marked with the same emblem. Beside it, a name: Albert Carr.

"The disgraced council chair," Amelia said. "He vanished after the rezoning scandal."

"He didn't vanish," Clara said. "He's back. And Harold might just be the front."

They stood in silence.

If Carr was truly behind this—if he had puppeteered the preservation narrative, the library board, and even Harold—then Eleanor's death hadn't been a warning.

It had been a silencing.

And Clara was done being quiet.

Chapter 25

Ghosts in the Archives

The vaults beneath Tumblebrook were colder than Amelia Farnsworth remembered.

Spring had begun to bloom aboveground—buds on the trees, soft light in the air—but down here, beneath the old library, time had stalled. Cold stone walls exhaled dampness. The scent of mildew, aged parchment, and something older clung to every step. It smelled like memory.

Amelia descended slowly, flashlight in one hand, Eleanor's annotated sketchbook in the other. The beam bobbed across crumbling file boxes, long-dead office chairs, and decades of bureaucratic neglect. Shadows clung to corners like reluctant ghosts, unwilling to yield their secrets.

Clara had offered to come. Insisted, in fact. But Amelia had asked her to stay topside—to continue coordinating with their growing alliance of quiet resistors: local historians, disillusioned board members, sympathetic business owners. Tumblebrook was turning, slowly. But this part—the descent—was Amelia's to face.

She passed through locked doors Detective Johnson had reluctantly unsealed for her, mumbling about liability and reputations. But there had been a shift in him, a flicker of recognition. She saw it in the way he handed her the access key. Not support. Not yet. But respect.

She followed Eleanor's breadcrumbs: marginalia scrawled in tight cursive, cross-referenced against sketches of tunnel blueprints and organizational flowcharts. Eleanor had mapped corruption like others mapped bloodlines. And now Amelia traced her path, step by haunted step.

In a back room lined with rusting filing cabinets and warping bookshelves, Amelia found them: banker boxes labeled with Eleanor's initials in thick black marker. Each one was a capsule of intent.

Inside, dust-covered ledgers. Meeting transcripts. Handwritten annotations flaring like alarms in the margins:

"Redirected without council vote."

"Oaktree Fund — link to Carr confirmed?"

"Same family names across multiple eras. Crosscheck with charter board."

"Carr's reach goes back further than expected."

Amelia sat cross-legged on the cement floor, flashlight propped on a broken bookend. Around her, the past rustled and whispered. Paper ghosts, tired of being silent.

She worked methodically, building a timeline Eleanor had begun and nearly finished. Money funneled from public trusts into shell nonprofits. Tax filings adjusted to obscure endowment withdrawals. Building permits granted under false pretense. The pattern wasn't just corruption—it was erosion. Quiet, generational theft hidden behind festivals and floral committees.

This was why Eleanor had been targeted. Her real crime wasn't defiance. It was clarity.

Amelia built stacks by topic: land use, trust misdirection, shell entities. She photographed everything. Her fingers stiffened from cold. Her phone battery drained. She didn't care.

Among the last files, she found personal correspondence—statements from retired board members, old threats rephrased as suggestions, silent cries buried in language that dared not accuse. And finally, a yellowed envelope addressed in Eleanor's unmistakable script:

If you've found this, you're braver than I was.

Thank you. Don't let them erase what was meant for everyone.

Amelia blinked back tears. She placed the letter gently into her coat and pressed on.

Then—blueprints. Rolled maps of Tumblebrook's civic zones, marked in red grease pencil. Each drawing revealed zoning loopholes used to devalue and purchase historic properties before converting them to private holdings. One wing of the library had been quietly slated for demolition. No public record. No vote.

Carr's name—his companies, his proxies—appeared again and again.

Near the bottom of one box, she found reels of microfilm labeled: *Charter*. She loaded them into a dusty viewer bolted to the far wall.

A black-and-white flicker. Grainy images. A 1980 council meeting. A younger Eleanor standing tall behind a lectern. Her voice crackled over the speaker:

"The library is not just brick and book. It's memory. Intention. If we let it go, we lose more than shelves. We lose the soul of this town."

Amelia closed her eyes, letting the voice wash over her. It steadied her. It made her brave.

When she emerged hours later, blinking against the afternoon light, she carried three boxes—each one heavier than the last. Across the green, the shadows stretched long.

Detective Johnson waited beside his cruiser.

"You were down there a while," he said.

"I found what we need," Amelia replied, and opened the top box.

Tax records. Board rosters. Signature pages. A paper trail as thick as a forest. The Oaktree Fund ledger rested on top, its spine cracked, its story complete.

Johnson skimmed. He paused. He flipped back, slower.

"This..." he said, then stopped. "This goes back decades."

Amelia nodded. "Eleanor saw the throughline. I just followed her trail."

He met her eyes. The last of his doubt faded.

"You willing to go public with this?"

"She gave her life for the truth," Amelia said. "I'm not about to back down now."

At his office, they spread the evidence across his desk like a battle map. Calls were made. Files were scanned. The county prosecutor looped in. Amelia wrote a full statement, sourcing every connection.

By nightfall, the first case file was complete. The foundation was laid. Tumblebrook would be shaken.

But ghosts don't go quietly.

Clara's text arrived as Amelia filed the last form:

Mayor just called emergency meeting. Two resignations. Flyers defaming Eleanor popping up. They're pushing back—hard.

Minutes later, a note was found slipped under the inn's door. Old library stationery. Unmistakable typeface.

Stop digging. Some history was meant to stay buried.

Outside, storm clouds pressed against the glass. Umbrellas bloomed like bruises in the square below.

Inside, Amelia stood alone. She placed the note next to Eleanor's envelope.

"Let them try," she whispered. "We have the truth."

And truth, once unearthed, had a way of refusing burial.

Chapter 26

In the Crosshairs

Clara Henderson stood in the center of Gossamer Fables, her hands braced against the edge of the display table like it might anchor her to reality. Morning light streamed through wide-paned windows, casting soft gold across the spines of old books and glinting off porcelain mugs neatly stacked behind the counter. The air smelled of lavender sachets and aging paper—normally comforting, but this morning it felt sharper. Edged with tension.

She was surrounded by stories, yet none offered sanctuary. Not anymore. Not when the real story unfolding in Tumblebrook was written in coded ledgers and buried council votes, not fairy tales.

That morning, Clara had done what Eleanor once did best: she had seeded quiet, deliberate truths. She reached out to the town's cautious middle—alternates, assistants, minor clerks, heritage committee members—those who had remained neutral. She didn't threaten. She didn't beg. She offered proof.

"You don't have to take a side," she said during careful calls and whispered chats. "But someday, you'll remember which way the wind was blowing—and whether you stood still."

She left breadcrumbs: a missing date here, a redacted line item there. Letting silence do the convincing.

By noon, the whispers had begun. The North Shore Gazette left a message inquiring about a private fund registered under Harold's name. Clara hadn't confirmed it—but she'd pointed them toward county records. The bait was set.

Back at the inn, she joined Amelia in what had once been a cozy lounge but now resembled a tactical war room. Blueprints, notes, annotated journals—all spread across the table like a cartographer's conspiracy. While Amelia drafted affidavits and coordinated with Detective Johnson, Clara transformed Eleanor's fragments into something direct. Human. True.

A letter.

"The library wasn't just a building. It was a promise—that knowledge wouldn't carry a price tag, that stories would outlive gatekeepers, and that if you wandered far enough, you could always find your way home again."

When she read it aloud, Amelia closed her eyes. Her teacup trembled slightly in her hands.

"You have to publish that," she whispered.

Clara nodded. "Tonight."

That evening, the Open Letter to Tumblebrook appeared everywhere.

Posted on community boards. Slipped under doorways. Tucked into hymnals, left on café tables, pinned to corkboards at the school. In the window of Gossamer Fables, it hung beneath Eleanor's favorite poetry collection.

And it caught fire.

Not with outrage—but with memory.

Elders read it to grandchildren. Teenagers recorded themselves reciting it. #EleanorsPromise began trending on regional social feeds. Local journalists called it "a town's reckoning in prose." The school board forwarded it to alumni. A choir turned the final lines into a hymn.

Even the skeptical went still.

It was a victory.

Until the backlash came.

The next morning, Clara found a thick envelope wedged under the bookshop door. Letterhead: Office of Municipal Oversight – Deerfield Region.

She opened it slowly, her stomach already turning.

A memorandum. Legal. Cold.

The language was vague, but the implication was clear: a warning. Any municipal official interfering with "pending infrastructure reforms" would be subject to review. The list of names attached weren't random.

Every one had supported Eleanor.

It was a weapon dressed as protocol.

Clara texted Amelia and locked the bookshop behind her.

Within the hour, calls started coming.

Pippa—voice shaking—said a man had been asking about her family trust. The town historian reported an unexpected visit from a Deerfield consultant. The school principal had been summoned for an audit. None official. All of it designed to intimidate.

They weren't just pushing back. They were targeting.

Clara returned to Eleanor's journal. One underlined entry sent a chill down her spine:

"If Carr triangulates with Deerfield proxies, they'll escalate to jurisdictional override. Don't let them consolidate."

That's what this was: consolidation. A final maneuver.

She arranged a discreet meeting with two neutral council members at The Corner Mug. Over steaming cups of tea, she laid out the evidence: falsified votes, shell companies, offshore ties. Detective Johnson was prepping a legal case. Clara needed their moral clarity.

"This isn't about buildings," she said. "It's about whether Tumblebrook governs itself—or becomes a postcard run by outsiders."

They asked for time.

She didn't have any.

That night, Clara worked late at the inn.

She digitized records. Uploaded documents to a private server. Sent links to two journalists—one local, one regional. Then she wrote another letter, this one for the future:

"You inherit this town. Its gardens, its stories, its unfinished pages. Don't let expedience erase legacy. Don't let silence write your history."

She posted it beneath children's paintings from the library: books with wings, a tree growing from an open journal, a stone path leading to a glowing door.

It spread again. Local news. PTA pages. Alumni blogs. It became a movement—not organized, but organic.

Tumblebrook had found its voice.

And then Clara heard something she was never meant to.

Walking home, she passed the municipal annex. In the breeze-way, voices. She ducked behind a hedge.

Two men. Familiar cadence. Low and sharp.

"We move next week. Deerfield's on board. If Tumblebrook drags, we override."

"Johnson won't let it fly."

"Doesn't matter. Once the buyout begins, optics are irrelevant. Sell them growth."

A beat.

"What about the librarian girl?"

A dry laugh.

"Let them keep their ghosts. We're writing the future."

Clara's breath caught. Her hand closed around the last page of Eleanor's journal in her pocket:

"If they come for memory, protect the truth."

She turned and walked into the dark.

They weren't just erasing Eleanor.

They were replacing the story.

And Clara wasn't going to let them.

Chapter 27

The Reckoning

Amelia Farnsworth stood on the cracked brick steps of Tumblebrook Historical Hall, her coat collar turned up against the late spring wind. The sky above was a bruised canvas of gray, and the scent of lilac drifted through the air like a memory trying to surface. The town around her moved cautiously, as though it too sensed what was coming—that today would change something permanent.

She had chosen this place deliberately. Not the inn. Not the library. But here, in a building steeped in the town's bones. A space that remembered before anyone else had started forgetting.

Today, she would confront Harold.

In the days since Clara's open letter and Deerfield's backlash, the town had begun to fracture in all the ways Eleanor had predicted—old loyalties eroding, alliances shifting. But the true battle wasn't public. Not yet. Harold thrived in veils, in backdoor influence and whispered assurances. Amelia's aim today was to crack that facade, to force him into the light.

She'd baited him with an invitation under the pretense of discussing a "heritage preservation proposal"—a flattering ruse designed to appeal to Harold's carefully cultivated image as a steward of tradition. He couldn't resist it.

He arrived exactly on time.

Navy coat. Polished shoes. Gold cufflinks glinting beneath tailored sleeves. Every detail screamed polish and control. But Amelia had learned that even marble cracks under pressure.

"Ms. Farnsworth," he greeted smoothly. "A pleasure, as always."

She shook his hand briefly, noting the practiced warmth in his smile, the clinical chill in his palm. "Shall we?"

They walked past glass cases of fading artifacts—black-and-white portraits, yellowed blueprints, a replica of the town's first voting bell. Above them, an old clock ticked like a metronome counting down to something irreversible. In the main gallery, two Windsor chairs had been arranged near the hearth. Sentiment dressed the room, but truth waited underneath it.

Amelia didn't bother with pleasantries.

"You know why we're really here."

Harold's brow lifted. "You implied you wanted guidance on preservation."

"I do. Of the truth."

The smile wavered—only slightly, but it was enough.

Amelia leaned in. "We found Eleanor's records. The fund diversions. The Deerfield memos. The shell accounts. Your signature. On several."

Silence settled. Outside the gallery window, she could see Clara standing across the street, feigning interest in a window display. Inside Amelia's coat pocket, a discreet voice recorder ticked forward, already capturing every calculated syllable.

"If you had proof," Harold said eventually, "you wouldn't be here trying to trap me in an exhibit hall."

"I'm not trapping you," Amelia replied. "I'm giving you the chance to explain why you sold out the town."

He leaned back, expression cool. "This town doesn't want the truth. It wants comfort. It wants assurances. I gave them that. Eleanor offered idealism. But towns don't run on ideals. They run on leverage."

For a man so composed, it was a damning slip.

"You didn't preserve Tumblebrook," Amelia said. "You rewrote it."

She stood. "We're not buying it anymore."

Then she turned and walked out.

That evening, she played the recording for Detective Johnson and Clara at the inn. Johnson listened with quiet focus, nodding occasionally.

"It's not a confession," he said at last. "But it's enough to blow open the public narrative. Combined with what you've already found... it's the matchstick."

Clara folded her arms. "It's time for the town to hear it."

Amelia nodded. "Then we go public."

A town forum was announced the next morning—a special joint session in the town square. The notice went out through local press, flyers, social media, and handwritten invites on bulletin boards. Under the canopy of a white tent, council members, citizens, reporters, and legal observers would gather to deliberate the future of the library—and to confront the civic corruption buried beneath it.

By the time the day arrived, anticipation had become a fever.

Harold arrived flanked by two attorneys.

Amelia arrived with a voice.

The square filled with residents, teenagers skipping school, retirees clutching thermoses, children trailing parents. Musicians played softly at the perimeter. The baker donated pastries. Someone brought lawn chairs and passed out blankets. The town was watching.

Clara sat at the front with a stack of indexed evidence. Detective Johnson stood behind a podium, calling the forum to order. His voice carried authority it hadn't before—his presence now aligned with something larger than protocol.

Then, Amelia stepped to the microphone.

She didn't shout. She didn't pace.

She simply spoke.

About Eleanor. About trust. About what was quietly stolen when no one was looking.

She described how public money had been siphoned. How records had been altered. How civic history had been rewritten to benefit the few. She listed dates. Named departments. Pointed toward patterns. But mostly, she told stories.

Of the kids who'd lost their literacy program. Of the widower who'd found solace at the reading group that was quietly defunded. Of the town Eleanor tried to protect—not because it was perfect, but because it was home.

"We were sold comfort," she said. "Wrapped in policy. Stamped with credibility. But it cost us more than dollars. It cost us our dignity. And now we get to choose whether we reclaim it."

The silence afterward was complete. Reverent.

Even the birds seemed to still.

Then a voice from the crowd: "What do we do now?"

Amelia didn't hesitate. "We rebuild."

The vote to freeze the library's privatization passed unanimously.

A formal investigation into Deerfield's dealings was opened by the county. A task force—co-chaired by Clara—was established to audit town financial practices from the last two decades. Several council members resigned. Others returned to their seats with renewed humility.

Even Sheriff Taylor, usually guarded, approached Amelia with a nod and said, "You brought them back."

That evening, the inn's porch filled with life.

Laughter returned to Tumblebrook—not in the carefree way it once had, but in the hard-won way of people who had weathered something and emerged stronger.

Children played under fairy lights. Candles flickered in windows. Neighbors passed pie tins and forgiveness. A harmony long buried began to hum beneath the bricks and beams.

The town had chosen its story.

But as dusk deepened and the folding chairs were packed away, a stranger passed by the inn. No one recognized him.

He paused at the mailbox.

Dropped something in.

And kept walking.

Amelia retrieved it hours later. One line, written in sharp slanted ink:

She was only the first.

Amelia froze. Her hands trembled.

Across the room, Lady Grey sat motionless on the windowsill, her amber eyes fixed on the street. Clara entered moments later, coat dusted with evening dew. She saw the letter and said nothing for a long moment.

Then: "It isn't over."

Amelia folded the note.

"No," she said. "But it's our turn now."

Chapter 28

Crisis Unfurled

Clara Henderson stood near the rear of the council chamber, her fingers curled around the back of a folding chair, trying to root herself in the present moment. The fluorescent lights buzzed overhead like a hive straining to hold itself together. Beneath them, the walls of Tumblebrook's council hall, once a symbol of hometown order and polite governance, now pulsed with a brittle kind of tension. The room didn't just hum with anxiety—it quivered on the edge of eruption.

It reminded Clara of the moment just before a kettle boiled over. All heat, no sound—until everything screamed at once.

What had begun as a hopeful continuation of the public inquiry —an extension of the momentum Amelia had set in motion at the town forum—had unraveled over the past forty-eight hours into a slow-moving implosion. Deerfield's influence had reared back with force. And Harold's remaining loyalists weren't the only ones who had emerged from the shadows.

Clara could feel it. The tone had changed.

No longer just resistance—this was ideology disguised as nostalgia. Theater dressed as patriotism. The town wasn't debating anymore. It was fracturing.

At the podium, a man Clara vaguely remembered from years ago—a retired shopkeeper who had once lauded Eleanor's reading programs—now stood calling for a return to "civic purity" and warning against "outsider influence."

It wasn't Eleanor they were defending.

It was a version of Tumblebrook that had never truly existed.

Clara scanned the room carefully. She listened not just to what was said, but to what was rehearsed. Cadences repeated. Glances exchanged. Certain speakers echoing each other's lines like a script.

Across the aisle, Harold sat with calculated ease. Not resisting. Strategizing. He whispered occasionally to his attorneys, scribbled minimal notes, and remained impassive as his name was repeatedly invoked. Clara saw it clearly now: he wasn't trying to win the town's favor. He was rebuilding a different kind of power.

"He's laying the groundwork," Clara murmured.

Behind her, Amelia nodded. "Then we dismantle it before it sets."

When the floor opened for public comment, Clara rose slowly.

She didn't raise her voice. Her tone was steady, each word measured and deliberate.

"Some of you want to turn justice into a debate about tradition. But justice doesn't run on sentiment. It runs on accountability."

Silence held.

"Eleanor Perkins documented every deviation. Every backroom deal. Every betrayal hidden behind a procedural vote. Her work stands. So will the consequences."

A ripple moved through the chamber. Someone tried to interrupt. Clara continued, unwavering.

"You're not afraid of the truth. You're afraid of what it disrupts—comfort, control, illusion. But truth doesn't whisper. It arrives with consequence."

She stepped away. No applause. No objections.

Only a brittle, reverent silence.

After adjournment, Clara moved through the crowd—intercepting questions, steadying shaken allies. But the change was clear. Support was eroding. Not from disbelief, but from intimidation.

A lingering handshake from the school principal. Avoided eye contact from the town banker. A florist she once considered a friend crossed the street rather than wave.

The support structure wasn't collapsing.

It was recoiling.

Back at the inn, in the firelit parlor, Clara met with Amelia, Sheriff Taylor, and two recently turned council members. The table before them was a grim collage of threats—typed letters, cryptic notes, one sealed in wax with the Monarch Society insignia.

Clara laid them out like tarot cards.

One card contained a single black feather. Another bore Eleanor's initials—then violently scratched through.

"They're not trying to silence us," Clara said. "They're trying to destabilize us. Keep us too scattered to strike."

Taylor tapped a note referencing a coded appendix from Eleanor's journal—a detail never made public.

"They know more than we thought," he said. "They're not guessing. They've seen the journal."

"They're not trying to bury it," Amelia said.

"No," Clara said. "They're trying to weaponize it."

Taylor stood, pacing. "They want leverage. A trade. Silence in exchange for surrender. Not justice—control."

The fire popped.

Then came a knock.

At the rear door, a courier from Maplewood Express handed Amelia a sealed envelope. She returned to the table and opened it.

Inside: a typed message.

You have one chance to do the right thing.

Destroy the evidence. Let sleeping ghosts rest.

Or the next storm won't be metaphorical.

Below it: a time and place—midnight. The ruins of the old bell tower.

Clara read it twice, folded it, and placed it beside Eleanor's journal.

"It's a test," she said. "They want to see if we'll blink."

"They think we're scared," Amelia said.

Taylor shook his head. "They don't think. They assume."

The four sat in silence, the fire crackling, wind nudging the windows.

Then Clara reached for her satchel—the one that had carried Eleanor's documents from the beginning. She packed the journal, the appendix, the letter.

"Midnight," she said. "We show up. But on our terms."

"And we bring the truth with us," Amelia said.

Taylor secured his badge and holster.

"No more shadows."

The others nodded, grim and resolute.

The storm wasn't coming.

It was already here.

And in Tumblebrook, storms didn't just destroy.

They revealed what had always been buried beneath the calm.

Chapter 29

Unseen Saboteurs

Amelia Farnsworth had always believed that towns like Tumblebrook didn't run on policy—they ran on rhythm. On morning gossip at the bakery, handwritten notes pinned to church boards, and the unspoken barter of favors whispered across porch rails. But as she strode down Main Street that morning, council brief in hand, tea gone cold in her thermos, she felt that rhythm buckling. The very fabric of familiarity now tightened into a warning: They're trying to unravel this before it takes root.

The Deerfield backlash. The doctored invoices. The whispered threats delivered under the guise of politeness. They weren't fragments. They were choreography. Someone was orchestrating a counterstrike—not loud, but precise. The kind of sabotage that unraveled quietly and left no fingerprints.

But narratives could be reclaimed.

Inside Gossamer Fables, the warmth of old wood, newsprint, and dust-warmed tea steadied her nerves. Mr. Lark looked up from the register.

"You've got that look," he said.

"The look of someone about to throw a rock through a glass conservatory," she replied, handing him the council brief.

He chuckled until he saw the heading: Budget revisions scheduled without public notice.

Amelia set her thermos down. "I need your help sharing it. Not just this page. The full story—who signs off, who benefits, and who disappears when questions get too close."

Mr. Lark nodded slowly. "Sunlight, then. Let's draw the curtains back."

Within hours, they'd broken the brief into clear visuals. Clara added a color-coded chart of budget discrepancies. Copies were posted in the bookshop window, the inn's lobby, and slid into every café bag with cinnamon rolls and black coffee.

Even Pippa began folding flyers around her tulip bouquets. College students created a digital thread—#ClearTumblebrook—and a slow, murmuring shift stirred in town.

Who authorized the abrupt closure of the arts program? Why were redevelopment contracts signed with out-of-state companies? Where had three municipal assistants gone—and why hadn't they been replaced?

Amelia didn't accuse. She connected. Let the questions bloom on their own. And they did. In book clubs and church circles, at barbershops and over garden fences, truth unspooled like yarn across the town's collective conscience.

But visibility came with cost.

At Thursday's forum, as Amelia stood beside Clara organizing outreach materials, Suzanne from the mercantile approached. Her silk scarf was drawn tighter than usual.

"There's been... a development," she said.

Clara's brow arched. "Go on."

Suzanne hesitated, then spoke quickly. "I believe one of my assistants—Paige—was bribed. She allowed someone into our vendor email account. A series of altered invoices now show donations routed under your name, Amelia. The amounts, the timing—it's been manipulated. It looks like you've been siphoning funds."

Clara's hand went to her pen instinctively.

Amelia's breath left in a steady exhale. "They're discrediting, not destroying. Undermining."

Suzanne nodded. "Paige has vanished. Phone disconnected. Her locker emptied."

They retreated to the inn's reading room. The invoices were meticulous—just believable enough to raise eyebrows. The metadata had been scrubbed. It wouldn't take much for a rumor to take hold.

Amelia pressed her palms over her eyes. "They're dissolving our credibility one line item at a time."

Clara looked up sharply. "Then we respond immediately. Not defensively—proactively. We frame it for what it is: an attack on civic clarity."

That evening, they issued a public statement through Gossamer Fables:

"When truth is manipulated, transparency is our only defense. Manufactured suspicion cannot erase the facts we've uncovered. We will not retreat from the light."

The response was immediate. Allies amplified the message. Residents re-posted it with their own stories of Eleanor, of local corruption they'd once doubted but now believed. But the counterattack escalated.

Sheriff Taylor arrived at the inn just after ten. "Unofficial meetings are happening tonight," he said. "Emergency votes. At the Deerfield Estate. Behind locked gates."

"Lakeside zoning?" Amelia asked.

He nodded grimly. "They're calling it historic liability. Eviction by euphemism."

"They're counting on silence," Clara said.

"They're about to get witnesses," Amelia replied.

She picked up the phone and started calling. Doris. Pippa. The baker. Even the antique dealer who'd long refused to pick a side. The message was simple: Show up. They're trying to pass policy in the dark.

By 11:00 p.m., dozens stood at the Deerfield gates, flashlights and lanterns casting the crowd in points of starlight. Young activists livestreamed. Retired residents handed out coffee. Taylor escorted Amelia, Clara, and two council members through the gate and into the lion's den.

The meeting room was sleek, corporate, impersonal—an affront to everything Tumblebrook was.

Harold stood at the front, gesturing toward a map. "—and by shifting designation to deteriorating asset, we protect our tax base."

Amelia stepped forward. "You mean you call it rot so you can tear it down."

The room went still.

Harold turned. "Ms. Farnsworth. You're not on the agenda."

"Good," she said. "Because I have no interest in helping you stage your legacy."

She dropped a folder onto the table—budget breakdowns, community testimonies, a list of falsified accounts. Clara followed, distributing copies. Taylor read out a statement affirming the meeting's violation of open access statutes.

Then came the community. A retired teacher: "I trusted this council. I see now that trust was misplaced." A florist: "You bulldozed people before you bulldozed property." A teenager: "Eleanor taught me how to read. You're trying to erase her."

The council splintered. One member resigned on the spot. Another recused herself permanently. A third leaned forward and, trembling, confirmed Harold had drafted the ordinance weeks earlier under a false name.

A motion was made—to halt all zoning changes until an open public hearing. It passed.

Outside, as dawn crept into the sky and the estate's lights faded behind them, the crowd moved toward the inn. Some walked in silence. Others wept, quietly. But there was no anger. Only clarity.

At the inn's porch, Amelia stood, Lady Grey at her feet. Clara joined her, paper mug in hand.

"The town held," she said.

Amelia nodded. "But we're not out of the woods."

A few moments later, a young boy jogged up the steps. "Someone left this," he said, handing Clara an envelope.

Inside, a single line: You stopped a fire. But you haven't seen the forest.

Clara looked to Amelia. "They're not retreating. They're regrouping."

Amelia's eyes darkened. "Then so are we."

Because in Tumblebrook, the truth had finally stirred the soil—but not everything that grows in darkness dies easily.

Chapter 30

A Gathering Storm

Rain clouds coiled above Tumblebrook like a warning—not just of weather, but of what was still to come. From her perch at the second-story window of Gossamer Fables, Clara Henderson sipped chamomile tea and watched the storm inch closer across the hills, veiling rooftops in shifting shadow. The light had turned brittle, the kind of pale-gray hue that made everything feel paused, waiting.

She wasn't waiting.

Where once she might have shrunk from this moment, buried herself in analysis and caution, now she stood inside it. There was no room for fatalism anymore—not when the town was waking up. Not when the people had begun to believe again in something more than tradition.

Tumblebrook didn't need protection. It needed clarity. And Clara had made herself the lens.

In the days following the Deerfield confrontation, Clara had immersed herself in what she now understood to be more than a conspiracy. It was a methodology. A system designed to disorient: weaponized nostalgia, obstructive bureaucracy, and the slow erosion of accountability that had reshaped civic memory into selective myth.

But patterns have seams. And Clara had found them.

She mapped everything—individuals, motives, legislative anomalies. She used Eleanor's records as compass points, connecting decades of policy manipulation, committee stacking, and procedural sleight-of-hand into a lattice of quiet control. Harold had been a face, but never the only hand. The real architecture of influence had long outlived him—and Clara now had the blueprint.

In dim corners of the bookshop, beneath the hum of pendant lights and the scent of oiled wood, she began to meet with people who once might have remained silent: alternates, aides, forgotten clerks. Some spoke in whispers. Others handed her documents. Many had never been asked before.

Each voice added another brick to a structure Clara was rebuilding from within.

Melanie, the postmaster, slipped sealed statements beneath coffee mugs. Jack Aldridge, a retired contractor who'd once laughed off corruption, brought in dog-eared zoning maps and permit discrepancies he'd kept in a drawer for two decades. Even the fire chief, long neutral, quietly agreed to audit procurement logs. Their stories wove a counter-narrative—one not of rebellion, but of reclamation.

And then came the artists.

Inspired by Eleanor and the cascade of quiet defiance, muralists turned alleyways into billboards for truth. A towering painting of a book splitting open to reveal roots took over the side of the old printing shop. Beneath it, someone had scrawled in chalk: Let nothing be buried again.

Clara worked late into the nights with Amelia, codifying not just what had gone wrong but how to fix it. The final product wasn't a manifesto. It was a town-wide reform package: revised transparency protocols, rotating civic oversight, term limits, and mandatory third-party reviews of major development projects.

Where once the town had looked away, now it leaned in.

The café posted the proposal beside the specials board. The church printed excerpts in their bulletin. Retired teachers gathered in circles to discuss it over tea. A group of teenagers hosted a livestream reading under the title What Would Eleanor Do?—and it trended locally within hours.

Tumblebrook, it seemed, didn't just want healing. It was ready to earn it.

The newspaper, long cautious, published an exposé series titled Unearthed Roots, pulling directly from Clara's files. The local radio aired late-night call-ins from residents sharing stories once held back by fear. Garden clubs began planning civic beautification drives. Children handed out homemade pins that read "Guardians of the Library."

By Friday, the council chambers were full. Not just occupied. Buzzing. The walls seemed to hum with anticipation.

Clara entered, her shoulders square, Amelia and Sheriff Taylor flanking her. She carried a satchel full of documents, yes—but more importantly, she carried momentum.

The young councilman cleared his throat. "Miss Henderson, you have the floor."

Clara stepped to the podium, placed her notes, and lifted her gaze. No projection. No theatrics. Just precision.

"This is not a manifesto. It is a map. A record of what we've tolerated. A blueprint for what we won't."

She laid it out point by point—broken procedures, duplicate entries, ghosted audits, backdoor ordinances. Each one sourced. Each one signed. No speculation. No guesswork.

With every page turned, the room tilted further. Not toward outrage—but comprehension. Clara didn't raise her voice. She let the silence between her words do the heavy lifting.

When she reached the final document—a ledger tracing falsified grant dispersals tied directly to Harold's past committee—it was like a pin dropped.

The mayor leaned forward, pale and still. "Miss Henderson... You've essentially written a new governance model."

Clara's voice was calm. "I've documented what failed. The town will decide what's next."

A breathless hush. Then came the ripple—applause from some corners. Shock from others. Pushback bubbled quickly.

One council member called for independent verification. Another demanded legal review. But the momentum was no longer theirs to stall.

The chamber ignited—not into chaos, but combustion. Energy. Voices layered over voices. Cries for accountability. Pleas for calm. The town solicitor tried to call order, but the moment had already passed him.

And through the swirl, Clara stood back.

Amelia moved to her side, brushing fingertips briefly across hers. Together they scanned the crowd—until Clara froze.

Near the exit, slipping through the half-open chamber doors, were two familiar figures.

One in a navy overcoat—the same she had seen in the Deerfield archive room.

The other: tall, stiff-backed, barely disguising their departure.

Clara narrowed her eyes.

They were still trying to vanish. Still betting on the chaos. Still assuming no one was watching.

But Tumblebrook was watching now.

The storm outside had begun in earnest—rain pelting the windows, thunder rolling in slow waves.

Inside, the council chamber crackled with a different kind of electricity. One born not of crisis, but of correction.

Clara turned from the door.

"We're not done," she whispered.

Amelia nodded. "Then let's keep going."

Because the reckoning had come. But the reckoning wasn't the end.

It was only the threshold.

Chapter 31

Temptation and Treason

The morning after the council's upheaval settled over Tumblebrook like a silent frost—sharp, clean, and quietly dangerous. Amelia Farnsworth stood before the inn's hearth, coffee in hand, watching the last embers shift in their cradle of ash. Outside, the wind stirred uneasily. Even Lady Grey, normally curled in cozy indifference, lay alert and still, her amber gaze fixed on the window, as if listening for something just beyond the glass.

The town had changed. But it hadn't settled.

Headlines framed the moment as victory—*Civic Reckoning in Tumblebrook* and *Henderson's Findings Spur Legal Action* —but Amelia knew better. The first stones had been overturned. Now the real excavation began.

While Clara held the front lines of civic reform, Amelia moved through quieter terrain: history, inheritance, and the fragile spaces where facts were most easily rewritten. She descended into the inn's stone cellar, where dust and silence had kept company for generations. With gloved hands, she unearthed Annie Farnsworth's ledgers —books passed down like relics, once mundane, now potentially revelatory.

Midway through the 1956 ledger, a thick envelope slid free.

Inside: letters. Correspondences between Annie and Eleanor—first full of anecdotes and bookstore gossip, but soon shifting in tone. Beneath the casual updates, urgency bloomed.

"They seek to alter not just our shelves, but the memory that holds us together. Archives are power, and they know it."

Another, written hastily in Eleanor's familiar scrawl:

"The documents are fading, but the danger is rising."

Margins bristled with initials, dates, and meeting codes. A record of resistance—half a century old and unfinished.

Eleanor hadn't merely fought back. She'd left instructions.

Amelia spent the day compiling what she now saw as a blueprint: letters, handwritten marginalia, deeds revealing buried endowment protections, legal language so precise it could only have been engineered for erasure. And it all pointed to a single truth:

Harold's proposed development wasn't just a land grab—it was a systematic rewriting of Tumblebrook's public trust.

He hadn't acted alone. The shell organizations, offshore filings, and silent votes revealed a conspiracy decades deep.

That afternoon, Amelia presented her findings at an emergency mediation held in the old mill's converted town hall. Representatives from the Preservation Commission, local historians, business owners, and press filled the room—some curious, others wary.

Amelia's voice was calm, her message unflinching.

*"*This is not about nostalgia. It's about consequence. Our records weren't neglected. They were erased—deliberately, strategically, and for profit.*"*

She walked them through annotated maps, copies of redacted motions, and ledger trails linking shell companies to known affiliates of the Deerfield Foundation. Each connection stitched a broader portrait: weaponized preservation rhetoric used to justify cultural theft.

The crowd shifted uneasily. Some nodded. Others stiffened.

Councilman Keene, quiet and evasive in recent meetings, approached during a break.

"You're turning sentiment into statute," he said, tone unreadable.

Amelia didn't flinch. "I'm preventing sentiment from being sold."

He didn't argue. But he didn't agree either.

And that was the danger now. Not loud opposition, but quiet retreat.

Back at the inn, Amelia and Clara cataloged responses, tracking who leaned in and who stepped back. Their lists had grown more granular—not just who could be trusted, but how far.

Opposition had begun to shift its mask. No longer denying reform, they now cloaked obstruction in appeals to "balance" and "respectful compromise." Clara coined the tactic the velvet dagger—sabotage dressed in politeness.

Then, a spark.

Students from the local community college arrived with a proposal: digitize everything. Every map, letter, transcript. Build a public-facing archive that would outlive whispers and outmaneuver erasure.

"If they bury history," one student said, "we'll give it roots they can't pull out."

For a moment, it felt like hope had teeth.

That evening, in the inn's firelit reading room, Amelia and Clara worked late, annotating their case for the next hearing. Lady Grey nestled near the hearth, purring softly. Between them, documents stretched like a quilt of resistance.

"You're doing what Eleanor couldn't," Clara said.

Amelia smiled faintly. "Only because she left the path."

It should have been a moment of calm.

Until a knock cracked against the inn's front door—followed by voices.

Amelia rose. Clara followed, tension rippling through her frame.

In the foyer stood three figures.

Suzanne Holloway. Councilman Keene. And a third—a man they

didn't recognize, wearing his Deerfield Foundation pin like a badge of ownership. His suit was crisp. His eyes, cold.

"You think you've won," Suzanne said, brittle. "You've only drawn fire."

"You've disrupted decades of balance," Keene added. "This inn, your reputation—none of it is beyond challenge."

The Deerfield man stepped forward. "This is not a threat, Ms. Farnsworth. It's a correction."

Amelia's spine straightened. "This isn't a negotiation."

"No," he said. "It's a warning."

Lady Grey hissed. Clara's hand went to the folio on the table.

"We need to move," she said quietly.

They turned, Clara grabbing the satchel of evidence, and slipped through the kitchen hall as footsteps thudded behind them. Out through the herb garden, into the woods. The air was sharp with pine and coming rain. They ran downhill, boots slick on moss.

Behind them: shouting. A flashlight beam slicing through the dark.

Ahead: the hush of forest and the promise of cover.

Under the limbs of an old birch, they caught their breath. Clara's fingers curled protectively around the documents.

"It's not just about records anymore," Amelia whispered. "It's about memory. And what they'll do to control it."

"Then we make memory fight back," Clara replied.

Moonlight filtered through the branches like silent resolve. In the distance, the lights of town flickered like signals. They hadn't been chased off.

They'd simply gone underground. Again. Like Eleanor once had.

Only now, they had the story. The proof. The town.

And each other.

The final storm hadn't come.

But they were ready for it.

Chapter 32

Reconstructing Faces

The rains came hard overnight, battering Tumblebrook's cobblestone streets with a force that felt less like weather and more like reckoning. Water coursed through alleyways, loosening dust and debris long settled. It was as though the town itself was being stripped to its core—its history no longer willing to remain hidden.

Clara Henderson stood beneath the overhang of Gossamer Fables, a cup of green tea warming her hands as she watched rain trace latticework down the glass. Though the storm had passed, its echoes remained—pools reflecting a bruised sky, gutters spilling over. Tumblebrook stood suspended, caught between what it had been and what it could become.

Inside, the shop was hushed. Clara's mind was not.

She had spent the early morning immersed in files: archived council minutes, Eleanor's annotated letters, and call logs from the library's main line. The patterns were unmistakable now—not only how Harold had amassed power, but why no one had challenged him. Until now.

At the heavy wooden table, evidence lay neatly stacked: ordinances, ledgers, Eleanor's memos, maps marked in red. She and Amelia had constructed a latticework of truth. The most dangerous thing about it?

It worked.

Clara's latest breakthrough hadn't come from a revelation, but from a detail—a quiet inconsistency. Harold's campaign biography claimed an "appointment" to a town advisory board. But the official records showed no such vote. His authority had been assumed, not granted.

She ran the inconsistency past Amelia and contacted the interim dean at the local college, where Harold had once boasted honorary affiliations.

The response came swift and loud.

Within forty-eight hours, the college publicly disavowed Harold, revoking his status and citing "persistent misrepresentation." The fallout spread quickly. But Clara didn't center herself. She directed attention back to Eleanor.

She built coalitions with faculty, librarians, and civic historians. They didn't just verify her findings—they fortified them, weaving Eleanor's records with academic citations and legislative analysis. What began as a grassroots effort became a town-wide reckoning— one citation at a time.

Then, a breakthrough.

In a long-ignored archive of the library's call logs—buried deep within the municipal server—Clara spotted something odd: repeated late-night calls from the library in the weeks before Eleanor's death. The final call, minutes before the alarm deactivated, had been placed to an unlisted number attached to a parcel registered under Suzanne Holloway's name.

The number had never surfaced before. Not once.

Following the lead to a cabin just outside town, Clara, with Lady Grey close behind, found a burner phone buried beneath damp firewood. It was water-damaged, but intact.

The texts inside were undeniable. Coded language, veiled

threats. The final message was linked to a secure line funded under Harold's tech grant.

Clara handed the findings to Detective Johnson, who brought in Sheriff Taylor. Neither hesitated.

That evening, at a packed council session, Johnson and Taylor presented their findings. Evidence was projected. The burner phone, authenticated. Then, in a moment of stunned silence, Suzanne stepped forward.

Her confession was halting at first. But it spilled free.

She had let Harold into the library the night Eleanor died. She hadn't known what would happen, she claimed. Only that he'd said, "It must look like an accident. If she talks, the town burns."

Harold stood still as the handcuffs clicked.

That night, the town gathered for a vigil.

Candles lined windowsills, stairwells, benches. Residents placed lanterns on the library steps and shared quiet remembrances—of Eleanor's book recommendations, her literacy programs, her tucked-away poems.

There were no speeches. Only memory.

Clara stood beside Amelia at the edge of the crowd, their faces lit by candlelight. She felt at once hollow and whole. She hadn't just exposed a crime—she had preserved a legacy.

"We've cleared the path," Amelia whispered. "Now they choose where to walk."

Clara nodded.

In the days ahead, resignations would continue. Oversight committees would restructure. The town would waver, debate, rise. But something permanent had changed.

The story had been reclaimed.

And as Clara looked skyward into a rain-washed night, she felt Eleanor—not as a ghost, but as a presence woven through every vow to remember, every heart turned toward truth.

Tumblebrook would not forget.

Not this time.

Chapter 33

Revelations in the Library

The storm had passed, and with it, a hush had settled over Tumblebrook—not emptiness, but potential. The town had cracked open, and in its exposed stillness, something beautiful waited to take root. The air smelled of damp earth and lilacs, as if even the soil understood change was coming. It was a breath between thunderclaps—a question whispered on the wind: What will you build now?

Amelia Farnsworth stood in the heart of it, nervous and electrified.

It began, as so many revelations did, with Lady Grey.

Morning sunlight spilled through the lace curtains of the inn's parlor, casting soft patterns on the floor. Lady Grey, tail flicking with purpose, paced along the windowsill, then hopped down and trotted toward the door. Amelia watched her, bemused.

"All right, then," she murmured, rising. "Lead the way."

The British Shorthair guided her through quiet streets—past Doris arranging scones at the café—to the library. No longer just a place of books, it had become the keeper of the town's evolving truth.

The doors creaked open under Amelia's hand. The familiar scent of parchment and purpose met her.

Lady Grey darted toward a forgotten alcove behind the genealogy wing—Eleanor's nook. Tucked deep behind the shelves, Amelia discovered a waxed-twine-wrapped box, pristine and hidden.

Her breath caught.

Inside: Eleanor's journals. Leather-bound. Dated by season. The pages brimmed with secrets, reflections, blueprints—not of structures, but of ideals. Memoirs, manifestos, coded love letters to Tumblebrook.

Hours passed as Amelia read. There were metaphors cloaked in parables, but also sharp truths: clear calls for transparency, unity, and resilience. Eleanor had envisioned a town unshackled by nostalgia and driven by possibility.

By afternoon, threads began to connect. Her writings described a model of mutual patronage and community stewardship. Concepts drawn from civic trusts, cooperatives, and fellowships—tailored to Tumblebrook's scale. Even mock proposals and annotated agendas nestled between pages.

In a hidden pocket, Amelia found a list of names—people Eleanor mentored, believed in. Many were now leaders.

By twilight, Amelia had drafted a proposal: a rotating council of citizens, chosen through nomination and random selection. Guided by principles of inclusion and transparency, it would decentralize power and encourage shared stewardship. Youth mentorship. Environmental restoration. Historical literacy. All rooted in Eleanor's entries.

In the days that followed, she circulated early drafts, held listening sessions at the library, and incorporated community feedback. The ivy-trimmed windows became a backdrop to civic hope.

She presented the final proposal at council hall.

The crowd was hesitant. But as Amelia read Eleanor's words—lyrical, wise, uncompromising—hearts opened. Dialogue bloomed.

Murals were offered. Students pledged to digitize the journals. Even skeptics leaned in.

The council voted unanimously to adopt the community-led development charter. Clara wept quietly in the back.

It didn't end there. More of Eleanor's writings emerged. Musicians wrote songs. Children performed plays. The library became a living museum of progress, with Lady Grey often curled on the podium like a sentinel.

Workshops flourished. Guest speakers arrived. Neighboring towns took notice. Tumblebrook became not just a model of reform—but of reflection.

One evening, outside the library, Amelia held Eleanor's journals to her chest. The sunset bathed the bricks in gold. Lady Grey curled around her feet, purring.

Behind her, a voice—warm, familiar.

"You found them."

Amelia turned.

Not Eleanor—not truly—but a vision. Memory cloaked in form. Radiant. Present.

Eleanor smiled. "You're ready."

Amelia didn't speak. She didn't need to.

They stood—woman, cat, and ghost—as stars blinked overhead.

Tumblebrook's future no longer felt possible.

It felt inevitable.

And with it came something greater than closure.

Continuity.

Eleanor's story wasn't finished.

It was becoming everyone's.

Chapter 34

A New Dawn

The sun rose differently that morning.

Where once the dawn had painted the lake in tentative grays, cautious and pale, now it poured over the water with golden certainty, as if it knew it was welcomed. Amelia Farnsworth stood barefoot on the inn's dewy lawn, warm mug in hand, the scent of cinnamon and clove wrapping around her like a shawl. Lady Grey brushed past her ankle, eyes fixed on the horizon. Together, they stood in reverent silence.

Tumblebrook had changed.

The weight of truth, once hidden beneath history and habit, had finally surfaced. Eleanor's death—so cruel, so senseless—had not been in vain. The town had not shattered under the truth's gravity. It had bent, reeled, and then—astonishingly—it had risen.

Resilience wasn't a word Amelia used often. It sounded too polished, too performative. But as she walked the town square later that morning, she realized resilience wasn't a speech. It was a quilt—stitched hands and second chances. It was in the chalk art blooming over the library steps, in the laughter drifting from the reopened apothecary, and in the small, confident voice of a girl reading

Eleanor's favorite poem aloud beside the statue they had unveiled just yesterday. It was in the baker who opened early just to serve coffee to the town clean-up crew. In the young boy who returned a long-lost book to the library drop box with a note that simply read, "For Eleanor."

Tumblebrook's tapestry was being rewoven.

Inside Gossamer Fables, Clara was reorganizing shelves with the fervor of an archaeologist on the brink of discovery. She had added a new section—"The Found Voices"—where Eleanor's memoirs, reflections from townsfolk, and restored local archives now proudly lived.

"People are reading again," Clara said without looking up. "Really reading. Asking questions. Annotating."

Amelia smiled. "You sound proud."

Clara glanced up with a rare, unabashed grin. "I am."

Together, they walked to the newly appointed Tumblebrook Council Center—once the old town hall, now humming with purpose. The air buzzed with ideas. An artist and an engineer debated mural installations. A group of teenagers pinned up plans for a pollinator garden shaped like a spiral. Every corner sparked with shared dreams.

What had begun as a defense against corruption had evolved into something richer: collaboration.

Not the kind born of convenience, but of conviction.

Even those who had once hesitated—Sheriff Taylor, the retired mayor, a few of Harold's former supporters—had begun offering support, not apologies. It was better that way. Regret could weigh you down. Contribution helped you rise.

Amelia spent her days listening, shaping, responding. The inn remained open, of course—now a nexus for visiting scholars, artists, and curious tourists inspired by the town's transformation. She hosted open porch discussions every Thursday. "Chai & Change," someone had dubbed it.

The name stuck.

Lady Grey, once the quiet observer, had grown bolder too. She now roamed the library freely, often found napping on the circulation desk. Children left her notes tucked into books. A small pinboard was created just for her—a rotating display of "Lady Grey's Finds."

And amidst it all, Amelia wrote.

She wrote letters, essays, reflections. Not all were published. Some were simply offerings—traced in ink and tucked behind Eleanor's statue. But it helped. It healed.

The town's connective tissue had been rewoven. Its nervous system fired differently. No longer reactive, but proactive. Initiatives bloomed—housing partnerships, intergenerational skill exchanges, traveling book wagons.

What was happening in Tumblebrook wasn't just governance. It was story. It was song. It was mosaic—vibrant tiles of effort and imagination placed side by side until a new picture emerged.

One evening, while reviewing grant proposals under the glow of the inn's reading lamp, Amelia paused. A knock sounded at the door. Clara entered with two mugs and a folded letter.

"This came in today," she said. "From the governor's office."

Amelia read. Slowly, carefully.

Designation as a Historic-Progressive Township. Funding approved. Partnership programs pending.

They would be studied. Celebrated. Emulated.

Clara set down the tea. "You did it."

Amelia looked out the window. At the flickering lamplight on cobbled stones. At a boy helping an elder with grocery bags. At the mural of Eleanor's open hands painted above the council steps.

"No," she whispered. "We did."

That weekend, the council hosted its first Community Harvest Celebration. The square was lined with stalls—artisans, bakers, musicians. A story booth allowed residents to record their memories for archival preservation. Kids ran obstacle races beneath streamers woven like ivy across lampposts. The mayor, now a non-voting chair in the rotating council, gave a speech not about control but celebration.

Music played late into the evening. Lanterns floated into the night sky. Wishes written on their rice paper sides glowed like fireflies. The scent of baked apples and cinnamon mingled with the distant hum of a cello. Children danced barefoot in the grass. Laughter carried across rooftops like prayer.

The town square filled with warm lights that night. No speeches, no agenda. Just food, stories, songs. Tears flowed when a quartet performed "Eleanor's Song," adapted from a poem she once wrote in solitude and hidden among her journals. Her words had become an anthem.

The final embers of the firepit cast shadows on the brick wall behind Eleanor's statue.

And for a moment—just long enough—Amelia swore she saw her there again.

Watching.

Smiling.

She reached for Clara's hand.

"I think she knew," Amelia said softly. "She saw all of this, somehow. She just needed us to catch up."

Clara nodded, eyes wet. "She believed in this place more than anyone else."

"No," Amelia said. "She believed in us."

Tumblebrook, reborn from fracture, now surged with collected intention. And as dawn once again stretched long fingers over the lake, brighter and bolder than before, it seemed to whisper the very same thing:

Keep going.

You've only just begun.

Epilogue

The Ink That Remains

Autumn settled gently over Tumblebrook, painting the trees in ochre, russet, and gold. The lake mirrored the season with quiet reverence, its surface brushed with copper light and the occasional ripple from a drifting leaf. The air smelled of apple cider and woodsmoke, and somewhere beyond the orchard fence, laughter floated—bright, unburdened, whole.

Amelia Farnsworth stood at the edge of the Tumblebrook Inn's wraparound porch, a knitted shawl draped over her shoulders and a pen poised above the page of her journal. It was quiet—not the kind born of absence, but the kind shaped by presence. Contentment hummed in the stillness. The kind of peace that had been earned.

Lady Grey dozed in the sun, curled tightly beside a weathered book of town history, her tail twitching against the pages like a punctuation mark. In the distance, children's voices rang in a call-and-response game that echoed near the newly named Eleanor Perkins Memorial Library.

Inside, the inn buzzed with soft energy—visitors from across the region sipping cinnamon tea in the reading room, asking questions about what had really happened that spring. Some had come for inspiration. Others had come to learn. But nearly all left with a deeper sense of what one small town had dared to do when given the chance to rewrite its story.

Amelia dipped her pen again and wrote:

"What we inherit is not always chosen. But what we leave behind — that, we shape with every word, every kindness, every refusal to remain silent."

She paused, reading it aloud under her breath. Then she smiled and turned the page.

Clara arrived a few minutes later, windblown from her walk through the garden paths now lined with copper lanterns and hand-painted stepping stones. She carried a package—neatly wrapped in brown paper and tied with a twine bow.

"For you," she said. "Arrived this morning. From the state literary council."

Amelia blinked. "The council?"

Clara nodded. "They're archiving the journals. Every volume. Digitized. Annotated. Cited. Eleanor's legacy will outlive us all."

Amelia took the parcel gently, her throat tightening.

"I never imagined we'd get here," she said quietly.

"Neither did they," Clara replied with a grin. "That's what made it possible."

The two women sat side by side, warmed by the late sun, sipping tea and watching as a group of students bicycled past, their baskets full of books and apples. A chalkboard sign by the inn's gate read: "Autumn Forum Tonight – Bring Your Stories. All Voices Welcome."

Lady Grey stretched, then leapt gracefully onto the railing, where she stared out across the lake. Her gaze was steady. Watchful.

As twilight descended, the town began to glow—porch lights flickering on, music drifting from café windows, and the soft rhythm of footsteps filling the square. In the library's window, a candle burned steadily beside a portrait of Eleanor—one hand raised, a journal pressed to her chest, her eyes shining with quiet defiance and enduring hope.

In the margin of the photograph, someone had scribbled in pencil:

"The future is a story we must all agree to write."

And in Tumblebrook, the ink hadn't run dry. Not yet.

www.ingramcontent.com/pod-product-compliance
Lightning Source LLC
Chambersburg PA
CBHW040830010826
48978CB00012BB/686